Solomon Foxly

A Story Of Family

Billy Haake

ISBN: 0692793267
ISBN 13: 9780692793268
Library of Congress Control Number: 2016916832
LCCN Imprint Name: Billy Haake

The quick brown fox jumps over the lazy dog.

To the real Noah and Eli

With all my love,
Grandpa

1

It was nighttime in Johnston County. Solomon Foxly was patiently sitting on a hill that overlooked Farmer Harrison's chicken coop, his bushy tail brushing slowly back and forth across the grass. His silhouette was cast against the light of the full moon behind him.

Time to move. He skulked down the hill toward his target, crept around the coop, and peered through the cracks in the wood siding. Behind his hairy face with its wet black nose, his clever brain was plotting.

The overhead light was still burning in the coop, and, through the open doorway, he saw a dozen plump hens roosting in their nests. He ran his tongue around his snout, licking his lips, and stretched his jaws in a wide yawn, exposing pure-white teeth and fangs. He moved away from the coop and sat down on his haunches to continue plotting.

Suddenly, he spotted Barkley, the yard dog, walking around the farmhouse. Solomon froze and watched.

Inside the coop, a large red hen was settled in her nest, sitting on three brown eggs. The hen was the most productive chicken in the coop, laying the most eggs and scratching up the most seed in the yard. If there was such a thing as an alpha chicken, this red hen was it.

The coop had nesting boxes attached to the side and rear walls, and most boxes had a chicken in them. Directly across the aisle from the alpha chicken was a white hen, the only white-feathered hen in the coop. For some reason, one of Farmer Harrison's granddaughters had nicknamed this hen "Alice."

Alice and the red hen stared at each other from time to time, but it was doubtful they had anything to say to one another.

Earlier that day, the farmer had come into the coop and taken all the eggs, as well as three of the hens, to where God only knew.

Fifty yards away, Tony Harrison opened the screen door of the farmhouse, stepped out on the brick steps, and poured a pot of leftovers into Barkley's dinner bowl.

"Come and get it, you lazy hound! You haven't earned a meal around here in weeks!" He walked back inside to help with the dishes.

Barkley had heard it all before. He was a big dog with a brown-and-black coat. Sad eyes were set directly over a large snout that could sniff out odors and trails with the best bloodhounds in the state. He was of mixed lineage though and had always been a bit ashamed that he was a mutt. As he saw it, his job was to protect Farmer Harrison and his family, along with all the other animals in the barnyard. And he did a pretty good job of it.

He knew his master wasn't really mad when he yelled, so he walked up to the dinner bowl and ate his food, his tail wagging slowly. He knew he was getting fatter and slower. He needed to take naps more often, and, when he awoke, he had to lie on his side awhile before rising to resume his rounds.

Still frozen near the coop, Solomon watched Barkley. The fox rarely missed anything, especially when hunting for food. He knew the hound was bigger and stronger, but he also knew that Barkley was slow and could never catch him if he fled with a hen in his jaws. The tricky part was getting in and out of the coop safely.

Since there was only one doorway, Solomon wanted to make sure Barkley wasn't standing in the middle of it when he needed to run.

He sneaked over to the henhouse doorway and peeked inside. It was a delightful sight for his hungry eyes: fat chickens everywhere and each of them sound asleep. Solomon's hunger and greed told him to act now. He padded to the corner of the coop and peeked around at the farmhouse porch. It was bare. Apparently, Barkley had finished his dinner and moved on.

Solomon decided he would make a try for it anyway, yard dog or not. He padded back to the doorway and stood silently for a moment.

With a quick breath, he lunged inside. Almost immediately, the chickens awoke and began a fearful squawking. He jumped up to the nearest nest. A white hen was sitting there, a delicious-looking treat. The unfortunate chicken woke from her nap just in time to see a frightening face with its mouth wide open coming straight at her. She didn't have time to cluck before the sharp teeth clamped down on her neck.

With the hen in his jaws, Solomon landed on the wooden floor and turned to run out the doorway. All the chickens were running around the coop in a panic, flapping their wings and squawking.

The red hen looked down and saw her friend in Solomon's mouth. As fast as she could, she jumped on the top of his head. Her sharp talons gripped into his scalp, and her flapping wings beat his ears and eyes.

The coop was a cacophony of high-pitched squawking, and the swirl of flapping wings added to the pandemonium. Solomon became momentarily disoriented and didn't know which way to turn. Then he heard the low, unmistakable growling of a dog behind him.

He turned around, and, through the flapping wings, he saw Barkley standing inside the doorway, snarling menacingly and exposing long, sharp teeth.

That dog moved fast! thought Solomon.

Never mind that now. Split-second actions were in order. Solomon opened his mouth and let the chicken fall to the floor.

Barkley charged with fury. With inner strength that was born of pure terror, Solomon made a tremendous leap over the watchdog's head. When Solomon leaped, the red hen jumped off his head and landed on the floor beside the hapless and quite dead chicken on the floor.

The jump carried Solomon all the way through the doorway; he barely touched Barkley's tail with his rear legs. He landed on the ground outside in a cloud of swirling dust and began running for his life.

Without looking back, Solomon raced into the nearby woods with the howling dog lagging behind him in futile chase. As Solomon ran, the howls gradually became fainter until he couldn't hear them anymore. He stopped to catch his breath and let his racing heart slow down a bit.

That was a close call! he thought.

He hid behind a tree and peered around, looking back for any signs of danger. Solomon was far from the farmyard and could barely see the tiny bright dot from the floodlight attached to the coop. He sat in the middle of the pine forest while his heart and lungs settled down. The full moon overhead broke through the tree limbs and cast splotches of silvery light on the darkened ground below.

Solomon licked his lips and tasted a trace of the hen he'd almost got away with. The blood whetted his appetite. Calmer now, he began planning a new strategy.

Barkley chased the fast-moving fox as far as he could but ran out of breath halfway into the woods. He stood at the edge of the forest and sputtered, gasping for air, and thought, *The scoundrel timed it just as I finished eating that big meal. I'm freighted down with too much food. I hope the farmer isn't mad. I can't believe how fast that thieving fox was!*

Trudging back to the chicken coop, he thought about the fantastic leap the fox had made over his head.

Where in the world did he learn that, I wonder. He's smarter and more agile than any varmint I've ever chased. It's going to be a job to catch him.

When he got back to the coop, things had quieted down. Farmer Harrison was standing outside the doorway holding his shotgun. Barkley looked into the coop and saw a chicken lying very still on the floor. Another hen was standing quietly over her.

The farmer looked down at Barkley with angry eyes and grimly shook his head. Barkley couldn't tell if his master was upset at him for not stopping the fox, so he just stood there, waiting to be scolded.

"That fox has killed his last chicken on this farm, Barkley," Farmer Harrison said with quiet determination. "We're going to set a trap and kill him."

Well, he doesn't seem to be mad at me, anyway, Barkley thought.

The old hound looked inside the coop. He wished he could tell what the chickens were thinking, especially the red hen standing beside the dead one on the floor.

The farmer walked inside the coop and picked up the lifeless chicken. He looked carefully around at the other chickens, mentally counting them, and then turned and walked toward the farmhouse.

Barkley thought the best course of action was to sleep in the doorway, at least for the next couple of nights. Lying down on his side and still weighted from the big supper, he was soon asleep and gently snoring. The chickens, sensing that all was safe now, settled down too. The henhouse was peaceful again.

— —

In the nearby woods, Solomon crept to within a stone's throw from the coop. Peeking from behind a large hickory-nut tree, he watched.

Solomon knew it would be harder to sneak back into the coop tonight. And the shotgun Farmer Harrison was carrying was no joke. Solomon had seen his uncle get killed by one of those things. It had been on a neighboring farm while his uncle was stealing a chicken.

The farmer had been waiting for his uncle with his double-barreled twelve gauge. He had caught the fox dead in his sights just as he was trying to crawl under a wire fence around the henhouse with a chicken in his jaws. The farmer had shot him as he struggled to get under the wire. Solomon had seen it all.

No sir, not me! Solomon thought.

He stood in the darkness, never taking his eyes off the coop. Barkley's large frame lying in the doorway meant there would be no more attempts tonight. Solomon turned and padded back into the woods, toward home. The missus and the pups would just have to wait until tomorrow, when Solomon could catch something else in the forest to feed them.

2

The dark woods were beautiful at night. People who lived in the hustle and bustle of towns and cities might think it was quiet, but Solomon heard all the nocturnal sounds going on around him, and he loved every one of them—the continuous buzz of crickets, the deep resonance of frogs, the soft scurrying of little paws, and the hooting of owls. Nighttime in the forest was rather noisy if you opened your ears and listened. All these sounds gave Solomon comfort and reminded him of his own nature. He felt at home.

He picked up his pace a little, wanting to get back to the family den and rest a bit before heading out for another hunt before daybreak.

Then, up ahead, Solomon saw light. Wary as ever, he moved from tree to tree to get a closer look.

Six boys, all dressed the same in some kind of outfit, sat around the glow of a campfire, talking and laughing while foil-wrapped ears of corn steamed in the hot coals. Two plucked geese were impaled on a makeshift spit and were roasting over an open campfire. The strong aroma of the birds wafted past Solomon. He watched in fascination as the young boys took turns basting the birds and turning the spit.

A grown man appeared. He was dressed the same as the boys. He stood aside and gave sage advice on the joys of roughing it in the forest. They called him Mr. Thompson.

Solomon moved cautiously from tree to tree, encircling the entire campsite to size up the situation. There were five tents. In one of them, the soft light from a lantern silhouetted the form of another man lying on his back. Solomon couldn't tell from the black form what the man was doing—he seemed to be holding something up in front of his face. Glancing back at the campfire, Solomon took a deep breath and closed his eyes in pure joy as the smells continued to drift past him. He knew the biggest goose would soon be his.

The excitement for the chase was growing, and new energy flowed through his veins. Timing would be everything. He boldly stepped from behind a tree and crouched down, his muscles tensed and ready for action. The man who had helped the boys moved away and crawled back into his own tent.

Solomon couldn't know, of course, that this was a troop of Boy Scouts enjoying the excitement of their first camping trip.

＊　＊

One of the Scouts, a pudgy young lad, stood up from the circle and turned the spit. "Corn's done," he said, "and the two geese are almost ready."

"How can *you* tell, Jody?" said another Scout, laughing derisively. "Food is *always* ready to eat whenever you're around!"

With that, the other Scouts laughed and snickered. One of them picked up a small pebble and threw it at Jody's rather large rear end.

He turned and yelled, "Cut it out, for crying out loud! I'm overweight because I have a glandular problem. It ain't funny either!"

"Yeah. The problem gland is your *mouth*," said another boy. "You put too much food in it!"

This comment produced a new round of laughter and more comments:

"The geese are for *everyone*, Jody!"

"We only have enough for eight *normal* people. Maybe we should have cooked a third goose just for him!"

Mr. Thompson poked his head out from the tent. "OK, knock it off, already. Leave Jody alone and let him do his turn. You guys are supposed to be a team, remember?"

Jody picked up the bowl of sauce with a sullen look and slowly basted the geese with a brush, turning the spit after each stroke.

— ~

The aroma was hypnotic. Solomon had to fight back the impulse to run as fast as he could and try to carry off the entire spit with both birds still impaled. Then he remembered his uncle Sly.

Patience, old boy; patience! he reminded himself as he continued to keep both eyes firmly fixed on the campsite.

Several minutes later, both men emerged from their tents and walked into the circle of Scouts.

The older man, the one who had been reading in his tent, said, "I can tell by the smell that the geese are done. Who's ready to eat?"

"Me!" said one voice.

"Me, too!" said another.

"I'm ready!" said a third.

The voices blended together in an eager, hungry chorus.

"OK," said Mr. Thompson. "Mr. Barton and I will supervise. Tommy, you and George get at each end of the spit and pick up the geese. Alley, go get the big broiling pan from the back of my Jeep. We'll put the geese in it and cut them up. Everyone else—Marty, Steve, Jody—you know what you're supposed to do, so let's get started."

The campsite bustled with everyone doing his assigned chore. Tommy and George carefully lifted the spit from the pronged supports and took the geese over to the broiling pan, fat dripping on the ground along the way. Mr. Thompson used a large barbeque fork and pushed down on the lowermost goose until it fell into the pan with a plop. The second goose, the big one, plopped down beside it. Everyone stood and stared at the steaming geese for a moment.

"OK," Mr. Thompson said. "Everyone get their mess kits and hunting knives, and we'll start cutting off pieces of meat."

They went to their tents and gathered utensils.

—⁓—

Jody was the first to return, so he was the first to see what happened next. A reddish-brown animal ran toward the campsite at a terrific speed and jumped clear over the campfire. It landed in a cloud of dust beside the pan and, in the blink of an eye, grabbed the biggest goose in its jaws.

It was so sudden and unexpected that Jody dropped his mess kit with a clatter and yelled, "*Holy cow!*"

Startled by the shout, the others turned around. Solomon had the goose firmly in his mouth. The other Scouts briefly glimpsed the scene before Solomon, fast as lightning, ran into the night, his bushy tail flying behind him.

"*Holy cow!*" Jody kept saying. "Did you guys *see* that thing? He was so *fast!* He jumped clear over the *campfire!* I wasn't sure *what* it was at first. I thought he was coming at *me!* I didn't even know it was a fox until he stopped to grab the goose."

For a while, all the campers could do was stand around the fire and stare dumbfounded at the broiling pan with only one goose in it.

—⁓—

Meanwhile, several hundred yards away, Solomon dropped the searing-hot goose on the ground while he let his burning mouth recover. He stood close guard over his catch, ever wary of larger predators who might try to steal it from *him*. A few mouth blisters were a small price to pay for such a fine meal.

He had done a lot of running tonight, but he knew he couldn't stay in one place for long and had to get back to the den as soon as possible.

After a few minutes, he carefully put his nose close to the goose. It had rapidly cooled in the chill of the night air. Overjoyed at his victory, he grabbed it in his teeth and trotted toward the creek bank where the Foxly family lived.

After traveling through the woods for a while and getting close to home, Solomon slowed to a brisk walk with the large bird hanging out from both sides of his jaws. He held his head high, cocky about his triumph. *Wait until the missus and the little ones get a whiff of this!* he thought.

His bushy tail stood up from his rear, wagging slowly. He was thinking of all that had happened so far tonight.

I almost got caught in that henhouse. Whew! A close call. Solomon shuddered. Then he chuckled under his breath. *That big dog is just too slow. It'll be fun to outwit him again.*

The soft gurgling of the creek up ahead told him he was near his own doorway. He thought how lucky he had been to leave the chicken coop empty-handed. If he had gotten away with the hen, he wouldn't have this fine fat goose to bring home. And it had been conveniently cooked for him!

How thoughtful of those people. They must have known I haven't had any cooked meat in quite some time. Solomon chortled inwardly at his own wit.

The missus must have heard him coming or, more likely, had smelled the goose, because she was waiting for him at the entrance of the little cave on the creek bank where they lived.

He dropped the goose in front of her and stood back in quiet pride, his tongue hanging out the side of his panting mouth. He had a wide grin on his face and his teeth gleamed in the moonlight. Yes, sir! Solomon was the breadwinner here.

The missus looked down at the goose and nuzzled Solomon about the face. She was glad he was home and happy to see his fine catch.

Behind her, Solomon could see eyes looking out from the darkened cave. Two small foxes had aroused themselves and were looking out at their father with awe. Their names were Noah and Eli.

They ran out and began jumping all around their father, licking him and tussling about with each other, full of joy at his safe return.

After a bit, they smelled the goose and eagerly ran back to their mother, ready to eat. Solomon and his wife began biting off chunks of the goose as the two pups ripped off the wings and legs and tore at the delicious treat. The missus was gnawing at one side of the goose while Solomon gnawed on the other, their snouts just inches away from each other.

They soon finished the goose. The two pups carefully chewed on the bones, making sure no piece of meat escaped their attention. Solomon and the missus stood silently nearby. They were proud they had taught their offspring so well and grateful for the pups' good health.

After a bit, they went inside the cave and lay down for a good sleep. Stuffed and tired, Noah and Eli came in and lay down with them.

All in all, it had turned out to be a successful night of hunting. Life was full and happy for the little family.

3

olomon's special gift was his ability to jump long distances. No other members of his family had ever been able to match him when it came to tremendous leaps. This ability helped him when he was hunting and running for safety.

The first time his talent had saved him was the night he accompanied his uncle Sly on the hunting trip that had cost him his life.

Solomon and his two younger cousins had gone with their uncle to learn the ways of living in the wild. The elder fox was the natural choice to teach his three young nephews how to survive. He had roamed the countryside for years and knew all the back roads and trails to travel in the search for food. He had stolen chickens from every henhouse on every farm for miles around. He was the best hunter in the pack. And since foxes were mostly nocturnal, nighttime was the best time to learn.

There was a full moon that fateful evening when Uncle Sly took his young charges with him. They traveled for miles through dark woods and moonlit fields straight to the largest farm in the region. This farm also had a huge henhouse.

The landscape was bathed in the soft silver light Solomon loved so much, when the quartet of hunters stepped out of the woods and into an open area. The henhouse stood about a hundred yards away, in the center of a circle of chicken-wire fencing about fifty feet in diameter. There were no lights, and the door to the coop opened into solid darkness and complete silence.

The foxes sat very still for a few moments. Then Uncle Sly moved forward cautiously.

Solomon was the oldest pup, so it was his place to follow Uncle Sly under the fence surrounding the coop. The two younger cousins were to stay at the edge of the woods and watch.

Solomon was nervous. He came from a family of carnivores and had been raised eating the meat of animals that his elders had killed and brought home. Ever since he was born, he instinctively knew he would also hunt and kill someday to eat and feed his own family.

Until that night, he had only practiced hunting techniques with his cousins around the safety of the den. Wrestling a family member to the ground and pretending to bite his or her neck was only rehearsal. This was the real thing—killing another animal for food.

But Solomon was a fox. The hunt was in his genes and pulsed through his veins. His nervousness quickly turned into the powerful excitement a carnivore feels when prey is nearby.

He crept low and crawled under the chicken wire behind Uncle Sly. Once inside the yard, they both stood still and looked around. Everything seemed safe. Uncle Sly had raided this same henhouse only three nights before and got away with an extra-large chicken that had fed the whole skulk. Nothing had happened, so tonight he felt confident that the youngsters would experience a good hunt.

To be sure, he padded around the outside of the coop, Solomon trailing close behind. There was nothing to see except a wooden ladder propped up on the back wall reaching to the roof.

— ⁓

In order to better watch the proceedings, the two cousins moved closer to the fence, but not too close. The young foxes sensed the danger and were ready to run at a moment's notice. Uncle Sly and Solomon disappeared around the back of the coop. For a moment, they were alarmed, but the dark forms soon reappeared around the other side and moved toward the front of the coop.

— —

Uncle Sly sat down a few yards from the open door. He remained motionless for a few moments, staring into the darkened henhouse as his three students watched in awe. Suddenly, he jumped through the door into the darkness so fast that Solomon didn't know what to do except stand still.

There was an immediate uproar from the chickens. The frightful sound startled Solomon, and he looked around at his cousins. They seemed petrified, with their eyes wide open and hair on their necks sticking straight up. They scampered back to the edge of the tree line.

The squawking grew into a loud frenzy.

Uncle Sly ran out of the coop with a hen in his jaws and bolted toward the fence.

Almost immediately, a booming voice yelled, "I've got you now, you thieving fox!"

Solomon looked up to where the voice was coming from. There, silhouetted in the moonlight, was the figure of a man standing on top of the coop. He was holding a long object up to his shoulder.

Solomon glanced at his uncle, who was struggling to get back under the fence with the chicken, and then quickly looked back at the figure on the roof.

There was a tremendous explosion, and fire seemed to leap out of the end of the long object the man was holding.

"Gotcha!" The man walked over to the ladder and climbed down.

Solomon turned to look at his uncle. What he saw shocked him. Uncle Sly was lying perfectly still, his body halfway under the fence. The fur along his back was ruffled, and a pool of blood was spreading out from under him. In the full moonlight, the blood appeared pitch black. What was most gruesome of all, and the picture Solomon would always remember, was the image of the dead chicken still clutched tightly in Uncle Sly's jaws.

Solomon looked across the fence toward his cousins and could just make out their dark forms huddled together at the edge of the woods.

Then he heard the man's footsteps coming around the coop and realized he must run for his life. He also realized he mustn't get stuck under the chicken wire like his unfortunate uncle.

He made a split-second decision of what to try, not knowing whether he could do it or not.

He ran straight at Uncle Sly's body.

The man yelled, "Another one!"

Just as he was about to reach Uncle Sly, Solomon made a mighty leap, jumping completely over the dead fox and clearing the top of the fence by well over a foot. While he was still in the air, there was another tremendous explosion, and what sounded like angry bees flew very fast over his head.

When he landed in the soft dirt, he didn't pause. He continued running to the tree line. His cousins turned and darted into the dark woods. Solomon made a beeline straight toward them.

In the meantime, the man with the shotgun yelled after him, "You're a lucky fox!"

The man went over to Uncle Sly, lifted up the fencing, and retrieved the bloody body. He slung it over his shoulder and walked back to the farmhouse, Uncle Sly's head bobbing back and forth, with the dead chicken still clamped in his jaws.

Solomon joined his two cousins, who had stopped deep in the forest and were waiting for him. The three of them stood close to each other while their hearts continued to beat very fast.

When they finally calmed down, Solomon instinctively knew that by virtue of being the oldest and having come so close to death himself that it was now up to him to lead the little group safely back home.

Solomon led the trio for several hours through the woods and over the moonlit countryside until they finally reached the comfort of the pack.

The entire family was upset by the loss of Uncle Sly. But the life of a fox was filled with danger, especially the dangers from other predators that were bigger and more fearsome than foxes, such as wolves, coyotes, and large felines. Even large birds of prey such as eagles could kill young foxes.

And, of course, there was always the danger from the smartest predator of all. Although humans tended to think of foxes as pests and regularly killed them for that reason, people still loved to wear the soft, beautiful fur foxes were born with.

For tens of thousands of years, foxes have hunted and have been hunted. It is the natural order of things in this wicked, wicked world and is understood by both predator and prey. So, the Foxly clan accepted Uncle Sly's death and moved on.

For months afterward, the skulk endured the humiliation of watching the farmer's son as he rode the dirt roads and paths of the surrounding countryside on his trail bike, Uncle Sly's tail dangling proudly from the left handlebar.

The first time Solomon saw the tail flying by without the rest of Uncle Sly attached, he told himself he would never get careless.

From his baptism by fire on the night of his first hunt and for the rest of his life, the rest of the pack knew how truly clever and resourceful he was. Solomon would always be looked up to as a leader of his family.

Although most foxes hunted alone and at night, they liked to stay close to the pack and other family members when they weren't looking for food.

However, there were times when a pair of foxes chose to leave the pack and move out on their own, the way Solomon and the missus had several months after Uncle Sly's tragic demise.

They were both mature adults by this time, and together they wandered for miles through forests and farmlands until they decided to settle down on the side of a creek bank in Johnston County. They dug out a snug den for themselves, and it wasn't long before the two pups were born.

4

Farmer Harrison's first name was Claude, but everyone called him Tony. He was sitting back in his easy chair in the den with the shotgun across his lap, watching the late news. The meteorologist was talking about continued rains in states farther north.

Tony was still angry about the fox and determined that the next time it came around, he would shoot it dead.

It's true what they say about foxes, he thought. *They're smart and fast. I wonder how he got past Barkley. Maybe the old dog has seen his better days. I ought to get a new pup. Me and Barkley will train him up right. Let the old hound retire in peace.*

He sat quietly for a while, half listening to the television and musing about how to set a trap for that blasted fox. After a spell, he went to sleep. Fortunately, his wife, Clara, came in to check on him and carefully picked up the shotgun before it fell to the floor. She opened the double-barreled breech and took out the two shells. After putting them on the fireplace mantle, she set the shotgun in a corner of the room and went back into the kitchen.

Clara was working late, trying to get the main courses, the side dishes, and the desserts ready for tomorrow. The church was having its annual homecoming dinner right after services. All attending were expected to bring something. As she did every year, Clara was bringing much more than her fair share because she loved to cook and didn't mind working in the kitchen until the wee hours of the morning.

Tony had brought in a dead hen earlier in the evening and told her about the fox. She didn't waste any time plucking off the white feathers and cleaning and carving up the chicken, and she soon had it in the frying pan. Poor Alice.

Clara had already fried three other hens on the range, so the picnic basket would have plenty of meat in it. She had also made large bowls of potato salad, three-bean slaw, and macaroni and cheese. Now she was putting the finishing touches on two pies and a chocolate cake. Her family and friends loved to eat just about anything she fixed.

She didn't have time right now to think about the fox, but she knew her husband was upset and was going to kill it, come hell or high water. She glanced down at the back of the henhouse. She knew Barkley was probably asleep in the doorway.

That fool dog, she thought. *I wonder how he let that fox escape.*

But soon she was back at work on the food and humming softly to herself, thinking about what she was going to wear tomorrow and who would show up. Her two grown sons and her daughter were bringing their spouses and the grandchildren. The whole family was going to church together. As usual, they planned to come by the house afterward and stay for supper.

The grandchildren were always a delight to have around, provided they didn't argue too much or the big ones didn't pick on the little ones. They had plenty of room to play outside while the adults sat around in the shade and watched them. And best of all, they would leave to go home and sleep in their own houses when the visiting was over.

Yes, indeed, Clara had a lot more on her mind than catching a fox.

— —

Meanwhile, the Scouts, under the supervision of Mr. Thompson and Mr. Barton, had cut the remaining goose into small portions and divided it among the eight people in the camp. It was delicious and gave the boys who had never tasted goose something to remember. The corn on the cob was cooked just right with lots of butter, salt, and pepper wrapped inside the foil. There wasn't a lot to eat, but everyone enjoyed the fun of an outdoor meal and all the trappings of camping in the deep woods.

The episode with the fox gave the two Scoutmasters an opportunity to teach the boys a lesson about picking themselves up after a setback and going on as best as they could. Continuing with the supper was an excellent way to show this. The men had good hearts and were truly concerned about the welfare of their young charges. The boys felt safe with them.

After dinner and a general cleanup, the two Scoutmasters took turns telling ghost stories around the campfire. Most of the tales weren't very scary though, and, as they were told, the boys just looked around at each other with a "So what?" look on their faces. Perhaps the boys were too old to believe in ghosts. Most probably, though, it was a sign of the modern age. Back home, the Scouts' favorite kinds of stories involved urban legends about maniacs on the loose who wore white masks and used axes, chainsaws, and butcher knives to fill the countryside with blood and gore.

The boys did like one tale about an eccentric old hermit who had buried money, gold, and silver in secret places not far from the campsite.

The men gave ominous admonitions about being on the lookout for wild and dangerous animals that hid just out of sight in the nearby woods—mountain lions, bears, and poisonous snakes at least ten feet long.

When the campfire was just smoldering embers, the boys covered them with dirt. That was the last of the chores for the night. It had been a long day, and the boys finally crawled into their two-person tents. Zipping up their sleeping bags, they continued to talk to each other about all that had happened that day. The conniving fox was the highlight of their adventures. Each boy retold the same story in his own way and described what he would do to catch the fox if it ever came back. One by one, they soon fell asleep.

Lying on his side, Jody stayed awake. He was the only one who was still hungry. He made sure that Alley, his tentmate, didn't see or hear him as he cautiously slid his hand into the knapsack lying next to his pillow. He retrieved a king-sized Baby Ruth bar hidden in the bottom.

Alley's back was turned, and he was fast asleep. Jody was careful to tear open the wrapper without making a sound. He ate every bite, with no thoughts whatsoever about sharing a piece of it.

After settling into his sleeping bag, Mr. Barton picked up his book. Reading in bed had become a good sleeping aid for him, and he finished only a few paragraphs before he put the book down, turned off the lantern, and began snoring softly.

Mr. Thompson had also settled into his tent and turned on his lantern to write in his journal. He had two young sons at home, and he was looking forward to the day when they would be old enough to go camping. He wanted to make sure he had described everything that had happened, especially the details about the clever fox jumping over the campfire and stealing the goose. He chuckled under his breath.

All the Scouts were city-born and bred and had probably never seen a live fox before. Losing the goose was a small price to pay for the boys to get a glimpse of what living in the wild was about. Soon he tired too and was shortly asleep.

The campsite was quiet and peaceful. The Scouts were part of the forest now.

5

Sunday morning in Branton City had started out bright and sunny, but a storm was coming in from the north, and the sky was mottled with gray clouds.

Sheriff Tom Penegar parked his cruiser at the curb outside his office and got out. He walked to the front door while wiping his forehead with a bandana.

I'm already sweating, and it's only eight in the morning, he thought.

He walked through the front door and went past the reception desk, going straight for the coffeepot. He filled his mug and said, "Morning, Courtney."

"Good morning, Tom."

Courtney Kruger was the officer on duty this morning and Branton City's only female deputy. Young and pretty, she brightened up the office with her smile and wit. She was also on her way to becoming a good cop.

"Anything going on?" he asked.

"No. Nothing out of the ordinary."

The sheriff went into his office and sat down at the desk, mentally going over some pressing issues facing both him and the entire county. He opened a drawer and took out a bottle of Tylenol, popping two of the caplets in his mouth and downing them with a swig of coffee. He sat still for a bit, massaging his eyelids with thumb and forefinger.

Then he stood up and walked to the window that opened onto Branton City's Main Street. He looked across at the bus station and the Main Street Diner and wondered if Millie was working. He glimpsed her behind the counter, setting out napkins and condiments. She was wearing a white blouse and those slacks he secretly admired on her. He watched her for a while and sighed.

The street was mostly deserted, but it was getting busy. Even with rain, it would be packed with visitors later in the afternoon. People would come from all over Johnston County to enjoy the city's annual farmer's festival. On both sides of the street, a few vendors were already setting up their tables and umbrellas on the sidewalks where fruit, produce, drinks, snacks, and crafts of every description would be displayed. Monday was a state holiday, and people would stay late into the evening to participate in the various activities.

A bandstand had been erected in the little park three blocks west of the station house where the student orchestra from Johnston County High School would perform classics to entertain the families. To keep the teenagers happy, a local rock-and-roll band would play tonight, although the sheriff didn't think the word "play" aptly described the loud noise they made.

He knew the coming rains would probably dampen the spirits of the festival, but in past years, rain had never kept most folks at home.

In his midfifties, the sheriff was a local fixture in Johnston County. Nearly everybody liked him and thought he had always done a fair and honest job as the county's top lawman. He had been reelected for most of his adult life because the voters knew he loved his work, and, above all, he loved Johnston County and the citizens he was proud to protect. When things were casual and friendly, everyone but the children usually called him Tom. When something serious needed to be discussed, he was addressed as Sheriff Penegar or simply Sheriff.

The major issue on his mind this morning involved the whole county. Several days before, his office and other municipal services in Branton

City had been put on notice from the state capital that a flood watch was in effect at the dam. It hadn't rained in over a month, but he was supposed to go to the dam later in the afternoon and meet with members of the local volunteer fire department as well as the mayor. The mayor had said the meeting was "only precautionary." There was talk of cancelling the festival at the last minute, but it was decided to let it continue as planned.

The sheriff had another problem to deal with today. It was Sonny Folsom, and the problem had started a long time ago. Sonny, who was thirty-two years old, was a son of Johnston County's most notorious family. At least one Folsom family member was doing time in the state penitentiary every year for the past twenty years. They seemed to love getting into trouble and causing everyone else a lot of pointless grief. They lied, cheated, and stole on a regular basis.

When they were kids, they were brought up to bully other children at school, and, when they committed vandalism, their father bragged about it. The sheriff had grown used to the Folsom family tradition and regularly locked up one or more of them in the county jail.

In the middle of last night, Sonny had been accused by several rural households of speeding down the road in front of their homes, driving on their front lawns, and firing a pistol in the air. They had called Tom, waking him up at home and complaining loudly.

"Well, I guess I'd better go out there and bring his sorry butt in," he muttered under his breath. *I am not going to let this give me a headache today.*

But after he strapped on his gun, he picked up the bottle of Tylenol just in case and walked out to the front desk. "Courtney, I'm going out to the Folsoms' to pick up Sonny. Again."

She shook her head slightly in disbelief. "Wasn't Sonny just released from prison?"

"Yep," was his short reply.

When the sheriff told her what Sonny had done, she smiled derisively and said, "Such a waste. Good luck, Tom. What is this—round fifty-eight or so coming up?"

"Seems more like eight *hundred* fifty-eight. I wonder how much money this county has spent for trials, jail meals, gasoline, and manpower on the Folsoms." He donned his Smokey the Bear hat and his sunglasses and walked out to the sidewalk toward his cruiser. Getting in the patrol car, he thought, *Thank God I parked in the shade.*

He put his clipboard on the seat beside him, pulled into the street, and headed out of town to the homes Sonny had been accused of terrorizing.

⸺ ⸺

The bus station across the street from the sheriff's office was a small brick building that consisted of a waiting room with several wooden benches and a teller's window at the far end. The Main Street Diner was through a glass door on a side wall.

Inside the diner, Millie was seated on a stool at the counter drinking a cup of coffee. Millie owned the diner. She had seen the sheriff watching her from the station window across the street and had self-consciously straightened her hair, thinking he might drop in to say hello.

During the week, a full-time cook named Jerry prepared the orders while Millie worked the counter. There was a row of booths along one wall and a row of tables down the middle of the aisle, so everything was cozy. The diner filled up each morning for breakfast, and, at noon, the lunch crowd was even busier. Everyone knew each other, and it was always warm and friendly.

Generally, Saturdays and Sundays were the busiest days of the week, with folks standing in line waiting for tables and hanging around to talk and catch up on the latest news and gossip. But as it usually happened each year on a festival day, people seemed to prefer to wander the sidewalks and buy specialty foods from vendors instead of the standard breakfast fare at the diner.

The crowds would not start coming in until the afternoon when people began to tire of walking around and wanted to sit down and take a break from the hustle and bustle of the festival. Millie had anticipated this and gave Jerry the day off. For the next several hours or so, she was the only employee and acted as both cook and server. She also sold tickets for the Greyhound bus that would stop later in the afternoon.

She watched through the front window as the sheriff came out to the cruiser. She unconsciously touched up her hair again as he drove off.

Millie was in her early fifties but looked much younger. She was tall and long-legged, with thick black hair sprinkled with gray that hung down below her shoulders. She was a beautiful woman, and the blouse and slacks she wore revealed her attractive figure.

She had been a widow for about five years and did not go out with anyone. The loves in her life were her two grown daughters and her three grandchildren who, together, seemed to fulfill her for the time being. But she was a healthy woman, and romance was not out of the question.

Men flirted with Millie in the diner all the time, but she was used to it. She knew how much to encourage them and when to back off. She gave a warm smile to each of them and this generally brought a bigger tip. Most of the men in town liked Millie and enjoyed playing the game with her. They knew she had class and wasn't a tease.

This Sunday morning was particularly slow, even for the festival. The only people waiting in the station were a pretty young woman and a little girl who was about five years old. They had walked in from the street about an hour earlier. The woman was dressed in a tank top, tight-fitting jeans, and black cowboy boots. She had been sitting quiet and still on one of the dark wooden benches, staring out the front windows. The little girl sat beside her, reading a children's book.

Millie watched them for a while through the glass door and finally got up from the stool and opened it. "Waiting for the bus?"

The young woman glanced over at her and said, "I beg your pardon?"

"Are you waiting for the next bus?" Millie repeated. "If so, I'm the one to see about a ticket on the weekends. Everyone else is gone."

"No. I'm not taking the bus. My car is parked outside. We just came in from the heat. Is it OK to stay in here?"

"Sure, no problem."

Millie couldn't have known at the time that the real reason the young woman wasn't waiting for a bus was that she was building up her courage for something else.

The woman looked at Millie for a long time, as though she knew her but wouldn't acknowledge it. The little girl continued reading, not paying any attention.

"It's a slow day, hon," Millie continued. "Come in and have a cup of coffee with me. Drinks are on the house. Maybe your little girl could use a glass of milk or a soft drink."

The young woman stood up. "That would be nice. Could I have a cold glass of tea instead?" She looked at her daughter. "Allison, sweetie, would you like some milk?"

The little girl looked up and nodded.

"Sure thing," Millie said. "The company would be nice right now. I'll even throw in a late breakfast if you're hungry."

"No, we ate before we left this morning, but thanks for the offer." The young woman picked up a small traveling bag and her purse, took the little girl's hand, and went inside the diner. She told the child to sit at one of the tables and read her book. Then she sat down on a stool at the counter and put her belongings on the floor.

Millie walked behind the counter, filled a glass with ice cubes, and set it in front of her guest. She took a plastic pitcher from the refrigerator, filled the glass with tea, and asked, "Your little girl's name is Allison?"

There was a slight nod from the woman.

Millie got out a carton of fresh milk and poured some into a large plastic cup. After she set the milk in front of the child, she took the glass lid off a display of baked sweets on the counter and picked up a giant chocolate chip cookie. She looked quizzically at the woman until she got an OK nod. Millie put the cookie on a small plate and set it beside the milk. The little girl looked up and nodded.

"Allison doesn't speak, but that's her way of saying thank you."

Millie looked with compassion at the child for a moment and smiled. "You're welcome, Allison. It's nice to have you here." She went back behind the counter and leaned across it on her forearms. "My name's Millie. What's yours?"

"I'm Mattie. Thank you for the generosity." The woman drank over half the tea before setting the glass down.

Millie promptly refilled it and asked, "Are you just passing through?"

"Well, sort of. I used to live here when I was a kid."

"Really? I've been here all my life, and I don't remember you. Did you leave when you were really young?"

The young woman hesitated for a moment, as if something painful was stirring just below the surface. "It was fifteen years ago. I was thirteen when I left. Actually, I ran away."

"Ran away from whom and what?" Millie's curiosity was piqued.

"My stepfather, mostly. I recently heard that he died about five years ago. I came back to bury some ghosts that have been haunting me."

"What was your stepfather's name? I'm sure I must have known him."

The young woman hesitated again, as if just mentioning his name was dreadful. "He was Axel Folsom. He lived...I mean, we all lived out in the country. My stepbrothers still live out there, I think. I haven't talked to any of them since I left." Mattie subtly stressed the word "step" when she spoke of them.

Millie stifled a gasp. The memories flooded back—the Folsoms. Of course! This was little Mattie. She had been just a wisp of a child back then, shy and scared of everyone.

Millie's daughter Kelly had once been married to Butch Folsom. Millie remembered catching a glimpse of a frail little girl peeking nervously from behind a doorway when she had gone out to the Folsom farmhouse to pick up Kelly and her infant son and take them to the doctor.

Millie had seen the little girl again a few months later. She wasn't sure, but it might have been the time one Friday afternoon when Millie had arrived and found Kelly on the front porch steps crying and nursing a bloody nose. Her husband had been sitting in a rocker on the porch drinking a beer, calm as a cucumber. Livid with the kind of rage only a mother can muster, Millie had loudly threatened to kill her son-in-law right there before the Lord and the whole countryside. She had screamed, "Butch Folsom, you lousy, worthless bum! If I ever come out here again and find you laid one finger on my daughter, you'd better have one of your shotguns ready if you want to live. I swear to God I'll blow your head off."

Butch had barely glanced at her as he set his beer down and walked into the house without a word.

Whatever possessed her daughter to marry one of the Folsoms in the first place always puzzled Millie. And the more she tried to talk to her daughter about the bad decision, the further she drove her away. Thank God Kelly finally came to her senses not long after the incident. She had packed up her child and left for good.

Millie's thoughts returned to the present. "You're little Mattie! Of course. You were very young back then."

Mattie gave a barely perceptible nod and looked down at her glass. "I knew your daughter Kelly. She was married to Butch."

"Yes. Thank God she finally left that crazy household."

"Kelly was always good to me. I wished I could have left with her."

Millie stared hard at Mattie, who continued her story.

"They weren't my real family. You see, Axel's first wife, the mother of Sonny, Butch, and Bobby, died. Axel married my mother when I was two years old. We lived out there until Mom died of cancer when I was eleven." Bowing her head almost as if in shame, she added, "I had to stay there. I didn't have anywhere else to go."

The two women fell silent for a while. Mattie quietly sipped her tea, deep in thought.

Millie stared at her for a few moments, wondering what Mattie was doing back in town. Millie was full of questions and started to speak again but decided to leave it alone and began tending to the various small chores behind the counter. Besides, she had known most of the story through the grapevine from years past.

The silence lasted for about twenty minutes. Finally, Mattie stood up and said softly, "Thank you again for the tea. I need to be going. I have some things to do before we leave this afternoon."

"Are you leaving this afternoon? Doesn't seem like a very long stay."

The less Mattie spoke, the more Millie's curiosity was aroused. What was she doing in town, anyway? She said she came to bury ghosts. What ghosts? In the back of her mind, Millie knew what they were—dark secrets many of the townsfolk had heard and whispered about, but, sadly, no one had ever done anything about.

Mattie walked out the front door, little Allison in tow. Millie watched them through the plate-glass window as they got in a dark-red Toyota.

Well, she sure isn't riding a bus today, thought Millie.

The car pulled away from the curb and drove down Main Street, toward the town limit. Toward the Folsoms.

6

Storm clouds continued to move over Johnston County as the Folsom household was rousing. Nobody had any plans to go to church.

Sonny Folsom was a nice-looking young man. He was about six foot two and weighed two hundred pounds. He wasn't exceptionally large, but he had farm muscles and was strong as an ox. He was sitting in the shade on the wooden porch of his family's house, eating a ham biscuit. A lazy hound of indeterminate pedigree was lying on the porch, and two more dogs were under it. A few chickens and a turkey were walking around the grassless front yard, pecking for food.

The house itself was a one-story wooden structure that was slowly falling apart. The shingles on the roof had dry rot and were coming off in sections. Several bricks from three small chimneys had fallen loose. On each side of the house, at least one window had been broken out and resealed with cardboard. Wood siding was missing, and paint was peeling everywhere.

The house rested on brick columns, and the whole crawl space was littered with broken lawn tools, empty bottles and cans, and mattress springs. There was a seemingly endless number of car and truck tires, and rusted pieces of metal spilling out the sides and rear of the crawlspace into the surrounding yard. Several species of rats, spiders, and snakes made their homes in this mountain of junk. The house would never be considered for Johnston County's annual best-kept lawn contest.

Sonny lived with his two older brothers, Butch and Bobby.

Five years before, their father had gotten drunk one night and killed himself by running his pickup truck into a tree. Sonny had mixed feelings about his dad. He had been a mean, abusive father, but he had taught his three sons a lot about surviving in the country. His boys learned the hard and fast way—if they didn't do something right the first time, Pa would smack them up beside the head and make them do it over until they got it right.

They were all expert hunters and auto mechanics, although none of them ever held a job for long.

And they were tough. Butch and Bobby had settled down somewhat and didn't cause a lot of trouble anymore, but they still loved to get drunk and pick fights on occasion. All three of them had been married, and each had children, whom they rarely saw. At some point, each of their wives had briefly lived in the run-down farmhouse, and each of them had quickly tired of the abuse and hard life. The boys almost expected it when their wives finally packed up the kids and left.

The house itself was filled with enough rifles, shotguns, pistols, and ammunition to save the Alamo had the boys been there with Davy Crockett.

Sonny had a mean streak in him, but it only emerged when he drank too much. He wasn't all bad by any means. He was cocky but not obnoxiously so. He had a wry wit about him that could charm, and he always had an impish smile that made others smile in return. He loved country music. And most of all, he loved his daughter, Sara, even though he didn't see her often. When she was a child and visited Sonny, she sat on the front porch steps while he sat behind her and gently brushed her long brown hair with his mother's heirloom brush. When he finished, he stood up and said, "Sara Folsom, it's time to take a trip."

Smiling broadly because she knew what was coming, she said the words her dad taught her, "Beam me up, Daddy!"

Sonny hoisted the little girl up on his shoulders and walked all over the farmyard, Sonny pointing out things and deliberately miscalling their names. "Look there, Sara, at that crocodile."

"That's not a crocodile, Daddy, that's a hound dog."

"Look! Over there. It's a dragon!"

"Oh, Daddy, that's not a dragon—that's a tractor!"

They walked and played like this for the longest time. When they finally felt tired, Sonny lifted her down and walked hand in hand back to the house and fixed whatever snack she wanted. It was Sonny's favorite thing to do with his little daughter and his most endearing memory of her. She was almost a teenager now and lived in another state with her mother. But the memories they had made together stayed warm in a special soft spot in Sonny's heart. This soft spot had been growing inside him since before he had gone to prison. He had a kindheartedness within him that he tried to hide with drinking and fighting, but he was getting tired of putting up a tough guy image all the time. The rumblings of change were brewing even though he wasn't fully aware of them.

Sonny had a few friends he had kept since childhood. Whenever they asked him for a favor, he generally accommodated them, even loaning them small amounts of money. Since a lot of his cash was ill-gotten in the first place, loaning it out was no big deal.

He and his brothers were fiercely loyal to each other, although they argued and fought often. All three of them had served time in the state penitentiary. Sonny had been released on parole only three months earlier. He had served two years for the aggravated assault of a city slicker. The slicker had been driving in the country and stopped by a local beer hall for a short draft and a game of pool. Sonny had badgered the man and finally shoved him. The city slicker whacked Sonny on the head with his cue stick. Unfortunately, the cue stick broke in half.

Sonny shook his head and muttered something that sounded like "Woof!" and proceeded to beat the daylights out of the poor wretch. Several bar patrons stopped Sonny before he killed the guy.

When the man recovered, he pressed charges, and Sonny was convicted ("Sonny pushed the man first, remember," said several jurors during the deliberations.)

During those destructive times when Sonny drank too much, he loved to fight and cause trouble.

That morning, he had come out on the porch to relax and let his hungover head try to heal. He vaguely remembered driving around crazily the night before, and, somewhere in his hazy recollections, he remembered something about shooting his pistol. Had he wounded or killed anybody? He forgot most of the details. He didn't let it worry him though. He ate the ham biscuit slowly and pondered what he was going to do later.

As he was finishing up, the sheriff's cruiser turned off the highway onto the long dirt drive.

Wonder why the sheriff's coming out here? he thought. *Maybe I did shoot somebody.*

He continued to sit in the rusty lawn chair until the sheriff pulled his car in the front yard and got out. Sonny stood up as the lawman walked over to the house. "Howdy, Sheriff. What's going on?"

"Well, Sonny, we both have a problem here." The sheriff was standing relaxed at the base of the front porch steps, his left hand holding his clipboard, and his right hand resting casually on his service revolver.

"What is it, Sheriff? Did I do something wrong?"

"Well, as a matter of fact, you did, Sonny. Yes, you did. Do you remember where you were last night about three in the morning?"

"Can't seem to recollect, Sheriff. I've got a terrible headache right now, and I really don't remember much about last night."

The sheriff put his sunglasses in his breast pocket and leafed through the pages on the clipboard, reading his notes. "I'm going to refresh your memory. Let's see. The way I've been able to piece the story together, you started out last night drinking at the Two Deuces Saloon. That, I'm afraid to say, was your first parole violation."

He flipped a page. "Then you started a fight in the parking lot with Tom Lazenby. Knocked him out cold. Drunk and disorderly along with assault and battery—that's violation number two."

Another page flipped. "Then, about three this morning, you got in your truck and drove clear across the county to McAllister's Pond Road and proceeded to drive across the lawns of six homeowners, tearing up the grass and deliberately knocking down several mailboxes. Vandalism and malicious mischief. Violation number three."

By this time, Sonny's two brothers had come out on the porch to see what was going on.

Sonny gave them a casual glance, unable to hide the shadow of a smirk. "Well, Sheriff, how do you know it was me? You said it was three in the morning."

"There were three witnesses, friends of Tom Lazenby, at the Two Deuces who saw what happened there. I called them this morning, and they said they will swear in court to what I just told you."

"What about all that ruckus on McAllister's Pond Road? Who saw me out there?"

"Ah, yes, Sonny. You see, you started firing your pistol out the window of the truck *before* you started driving on the lawns. Bad timing. Five of the homeowners woke up and went out on their front porches and saw everything. Three of them were able to get your license tag number. They called me about three thirty this morning, all of them in a foul mood. So illegal possession of a firearm by a convicted felon and brandishing a weapon to the terror of the people. That's number four and a major violation of parole."

Sonny, summing up all the arrogance he could muster, put his hands on his hips. "Well, what are you going to do about it?"

The sheriff also put his hands on his hips, his right hand resting lightly on his pistol. He never stopped looking straight in the young man's face. "Well, Sonny, what do you *think* I'm going to do about it? I'm out here to arrest you and put you in the county jail."

Perhaps Sonny's hangover had dulled his common sense. He looked over at his brothers with a sly grin. "Well, Sheriff, suppose I don't feel like going down to the jail today?"

Sonny's brothers, however, stood motionless.

The sheriff continued to look Sonny straight in the eyes for a long moment. Then he glanced briefly at the other two and said, "You know, Sonny, I've known you and Butch and Bobby since you were little kids. I knew your daddy, Axel, as well. I know all of you love trouble and love to fight. You love to see the red blood flow. I've taken every one of you to jail before. You all know that I'm the law in this county."

The sheriff stood quietly for a moment. Then, in a voice as cool and smooth as a cobra's skin, he said, "You might not be thinking too clearly right now, Sonny, what with all that liquor you had last night. So I'm going to give you two choices. Number one. You can come down off the porch, walk over to the cruiser, and get in the back seat like a gentleman." He paused, never taking his eyes off Sonny.

"Or, number two. I'm going to *shoot* you, and then *I'll* put you in the back seat like a gentleman." Still staring, he turned deadly serious. "You're under arrest, Sonny. I'm taking you in one way or another, and that's a fact."

Sonny looked at his brothers, and when he realized they weren't going to interfere, he turned back with a wry smile. "Now, Sheriff, what was that first choice again?"

Sonny knew the procedure well. He walked down the steps, turned his back as the sheriff cuffed him, and got in the back seat of the police car. The sheriff got in the front, and they started off toward town. Through the mesh wire screen between the two seats, Sonny said playfully, "All right, driver, start the meter. I've got a lot of business to attend to, and time's a-wasting."

It had begun to drizzle.

The sheriff played along. "Mr. Folsom, the meter's been turned off. This trip is on the house."

He turned on the windshield wipers and headed back to town.

After the cruiser drove out of sight, Butch said, "I'm going to get my rifle."

"Are you going to break him out of jail?" Bobby replied with a sneer.

"Nope. Going hunting." Butch walked back in the house.

"I'm going with you," Bobby hollered after him. "How about fetching out my twelve gauge and a box of shells?"

As the two men gathered their gear and started out on the hunt, they were unaware of a pair of eyes that had been watching them from behind the barn.

7

At midmorning, the Scouts had already roused from their tents and were fixing pancakes and eggs over the reconstituted campfire. The sky was turning gray, but it had not yet begun to rain.

Each Scout was using his own portable kit of cooking utensils, and the small, compact size of the frying pans made things tricky. Most of the boys were getting the hang of it, but Jody couldn't seem to stop everything from sticking to the pan and burning. He picked up the plastic bowl he had used to prepare the pancake mix and dipped his spoon in it. He had just put a large quantity of the mix in his mouth when Mr. Barton walked over.

"Hungry then, are you, Jody?"

Jody looked sheepishly at the Scoutmaster. He couldn't speak with all the sweet mush crammed in his mouth, so he just nodded his head.

Mr. Barton, his hands entwined behind his back, looked at the young boy for a long time, and then gave a little shake of his head and moved on to the more successful cooks.

Jody finally swallowed the mix and stood motionless for a while. Then his hunger took over again. He glanced furtively at Mr. Barton, whose back was to him. Using the spoon and his fingers, Jody hurriedly cleaned out the rest of the mix and stuffed it in his mouth.

He set the bowl down and began licking his fingers when he heard something in the woods. He looked toward the sound. Just past the two SUVs parked fifty yards away, a huge black bear was lumbering through the woods toward the campsite.

Jody stood petrified. He finally yelled, "*Bear!* A bear's coming!" Then he turned and ran past the other boys out of the clearing toward the woods. He couldn't run to the safety of the SUVs because the bear was extremely fast. It had emerged from the trees and was now between the cars and the campers.

Jody reached the tree line and hid behind a tall pine. Still breathing hard, he nervously peered out and saw that everyone, including the two Scoutmasters, was running helter-skelter into the woods too.

Mr. Barton and Mr. Thompson hurriedly corralled the Scouts behind them for protection. With all hearts pounding, they watched from behind trees as the drama unfolded.

Normally, black bears subsist mainly on wild berries and vegetation and will avoid approaching a noisy or crowded campsite unless extreme hunger drives them to it. This black bear was obviously very hungry and dared to attack the food supply. Now inside the perimeter of the campsite, it stood up on its hind legs and looked around at the campfire and the nearby tents. It wrinkled its nose, sniffing the air, and then let out a loud growl. Soon, two small black cubs came scampering out of the woods and stood with their mother. She went back down on all fours and roamed into the camp, nosing around the hastily dropped mess kits. Half-cooked eggs, pancakes, bacon, and oatmeal were scattered about, ready for plunder. The bear cubs had wasted no time in joining their mother, and the three of them began eating everything in sight.

Around the fire, sticks had been stuck in the ground at an angle so that slices of bread could be toasted over the flames. The toast, burned to a crisp by this time, was left untouched by the bears, who were apparently afraid of the fire.

The Scouts watched nervously from behind the trees, helpless to do anything. The bears finished the breakfast foods. The mother walked over to Mr. Thompson's tent and nosed her way inside.

Peering from behind a tree, Mr. Thompson closed his eyes tight and wrinkled up his face.

Oh no! he thought. *God help my journal.*

The tent moved back and forth for a few moments, and then the bear backed out. No food in there. She moved from tent to tent with the same results until she went into Jody's tent. This time, she backed out with his knapsack in her mouth. She dropped it on the ground and tore at it with teeth and claws. She ripped it open and stuck her nose inside. With the knapsack over her snout, she raised her head straight up in the air. Several king-sized candy bars, a half-dozen honey buns, and a small box of powdered doughnuts fell in a pile on the ground. She shook her head violently from side to side, and the knapsack flew off. The cubs ran over, and they all ripped and tore their way into the various sweet treats.

All the Scouts saw what was happening. The revelation of Jody's secret stash was shocking in an amusing way. This caused several Scouts to lose some of their fear of the bears, and they began taunting the hapless Jody.

"Hey, Jody! You must really have a sweet tooth."

"Yeah, and it's the size of an elephant's tusk."

Even the two Scoutmasters laughed.

Jody, realizing he had been found out, tried to save face and yelled, "I was going to share all that stuff with you guys. Honest I was, really. Scouts' honor!"

The "Scouts' honor" was so lame and unconvincing that it brought a new round of taunts.

"Yeah, Jody. On my honor, I will do my best to do my duty to God and my country—and then eat everything in sight!" one of the Scouts snickered.

Jody had grown up with people teasing him about his weight, so he generally had a thick hide about it. But today something finally snapped.

Maybe it was because he was away from home. Maybe it was the primitive conditions of the camping. Maybe he was just plain tired and hungry.

It was probably a lifetime of embarrassing and demeaning remarks, remarks that he knew were true on the surface but deep down did not really describe what he thought of himself.

Whatever it was, Jody had reached his breaking point. Rage against the whole world—bears, Scouts, anyone and everyone who had derided his weight—boiled up inside him. He clenched his fists so tightly the knuckles turned white. His face was crimson, and he had a frightening snarl on his lips.

He jumped out from behind the Scoutmasters and began running at the bears, screaming at the top of his lungs. *"Leave my knapsack alone! Leave my stuff alone!"* Tears of anger streamed down his face by the time he got to the campfire.

Both Scoutmasters and some of the boys yelled at him to come back, fearful for his life.

Jody picked up one of the stones encircling the site and threw it as hard as he could at the bears. It hit the mother on the side. She turned an angry face and started to charge him. He threw another stone, hitting her square on the nose. The bear stopped, but Jody was unstoppable. He picked up stones and threw them as hard and as fast as he could. Not only was he standing his ground, but he was actually moving toward the animal.

Rage and inner pain filled him with fearless determination. And he couldn't seem to miss his target—every stone clobbered the mother bear in the head.

Unbelievably, the bear apparently had enough and sensed that she was dealing with something that wasn't going to quit. She turned tail and lumbered back into the woods, the two cubs scampering after her.

Jody ran after her and threw another stone. When he saw that the bears really were running away from him, he walked back to the campsite and stood by his knapsack crying, letting a lifetime of frustration flow freely down his cheeks. He didn't notice the other Scouts cautiously walking back to the tents.

Mr. Thompson came up and put his hand on Jody's shoulder. Neither of them spoke.

Mr. Barton walked up and said, "That was courageous, Jody. Maybe a little foolhardy, but it took a lot of guts to do that."

Jody looked in Mr. Barton's eyes with an almost defiant glare and barely nodded his head in acknowledgment.

Mr. Barton turned and said to the other Scouts in a loud voice, "OK, guys. I guess we can all agree the camping trip is over. Let's start cleaning up and packing it in."

Mr. Thompson squeezed Jody's shoulder and went to his tent. Jody walked to his tent and began retrieving his gear, setting it on the ground outside.

Alley came over and quietly waited until Jody had finished before getting his own stuff. Normally, he would have barged into the tent before Jody had finished. But not today, not after what had just happened.

Jody began rolling up his sleeping bag.

"That was great, Jody. Thanks for saving the campsite." Alley spoke in a tone that Jody had never heard before when people addressed him. It was the tone of respect, and it was wonderful to hear.

Jody's thank-you was a quiet nod of his head. Without further talk, the two of them began securing their gear and dismantling the tent together.

As they cleared up the strewn equipment and clothing, Alley spotted a Baby Ruth bar that hadn't been touched by the bears. He picked it up and handed it to Jody.

Jody looked at the bright red, white, and blue package in his hand for a few moments, deep in thought. Alley looked on with curiosity. Finally, Jody spoke. "I want you to have this Baby Ruth."

"That's OK, Jody. You keep it."

"No, really, Alley. It would mean a lot if you would let me share it with you."

The two young Scouts looked at each other, and suddenly Alley understood. He reached out and took the candy. "Sure, Jody. Thanks. I like Baby Ruths."

In about thirty minutes, the campsite was completely cleaned up, and all the gear had been stowed into the SUVs.

Jody told Mr. Thompson he had to go to the bathroom before they left. He walked into the woods and was standing behind a tree when he looked out in the forest. He did a double take and looked again.

No, it wasn't his imagination. Sitting about thirty feet away was that fox from last night, calmly watching him. Its long tail slowly brushed back and forth on the ground behind it. They looked each other in the eyes for a long moment.

After zipping his pants, Jody winked at the fox and gave it a thumbs-up sign. Then he walked proudly back to the SUVs and got in Mr. Thompson's Jeep.

It was drizzling as the vehicles pulled away. Jody glanced back and watched the dwindling figure of the fox receding in the distance.

In a few minutes, there was no trace of the Scouts except for the freshly turned earth where the remains of the campfire had been safely buried.

8

arly in the morning, before the Scouts had started breakfast, Solomon had been sitting in the woods watching the campsite. He had smelled the bears approaching and had cautiously hidden himself in the woods at a safe distance. A bear loves all kinds of meat, and fox meat was no exception.

Solomon watched the drama of the bear attack and waited patiently while the Scouts packed up and left. When the vehicles were out of sight, he trotted into the clearing and carefully searched every inch of the site, sniffing for any scrap of food that had been overlooked by the people or the bears. Nothing.

He thought, *Well, I guess I'd better start planning how to get a nice fat hen for tonight.*

He ran back into the forest, beginning the long trek toward the Harrison chicken coop.

Later, as Solomon neared the farm, he saw two men walking slowly through the woods, intently looking in all directions. Solomon froze.

As the men got closer, he saw the guns they were carrying. His heart raced, and he quickly crouched down in the grass behind a tree. He was so low to the ground that his eyes were at the level of the grass tops, just barely looking over. The men didn't notice him as they continued moving through the woods and out of sight.

Whew! thought Solomon.

Remembering Uncle Sly's fate, he curled his tail tightly against his side. He didn't move for quite some time until he could no longer hear any sounds from the men. He finally stood up and peered carefully in the direction they had gone. They were nowhere to be seen. Boldly, he walked toward Farmer Harrison's.

A light rain had started.

An open field was between the woods and the farm. It had recently been plowed and was crossed with deep furrows. Solomon moved cautiously, crouching low in each furrow for a moment before moving on to the next. Halfway across, several gunshots came from the direction the two men had taken.

Solomon peeked over the rim of plowed earth he was hidden by. A large deer sprinted across the field in his direction.

There were more gunshots. The deer's front legs suddenly buckled, and it fell to the ground about fifty feet away from him. The deer rolled on its side and gave Solomon a mournful stare before it let out a large breath and then lay still. Its dark eyes glazed over, and Solomon knew it was dead.

The two men emerged from the woods and stood at the edge of the field.

"I got her, Bobby! Running like the wind, and I still got her!"

"Hold on there, Brother Butch. I ain't so sure it was your shooting at all. I fired some shots too, you know."

"You're crazy."

The two brothers ran across the field toward the deer. Solomon had to stay low and hope they didn't spot him. An open field made him an easy target if he tried to make a run for it.

Butch and Bobby reached the body and poked at it here and there, trying to determine where it had been shot. It was a doe, and, in this part of the state, it was illegal to shoot does except on specific days of the hunting season. Today wasn't one of those days.

The two men glanced around furtively, wondering if anyone had witnessed their crime. The deer's thick black tongue drooped from the side of its mouth. Butch grasped the doe around the neck with both arms. With a grunt, he turned it over on the other side.

"Here it is, Bobby. Look for yourself. I hit her right there above the shoulder." Butch pointed at a small, bloody hole. "Your shotgun didn't hit a blessed thing."

"Well, I guess you're right about that. How are we going to get this thing back home?" The deer was too heavy for them to carry all the way back to their own house, several miles away.

"Hey, ain't this Ol' Man Harrison's property?" Butch asked. "If he finds out we were poaching on his land, he'll have us in the same cell with Sonny before the sun sets."

Bobby replied, "Yeah. Listen. I just thought of something. The power company's right-of-way is on the other side of that tree line. We can leave the carcass here until tonight, drive the truck onto the right-of-way, and drag the deer over to it. As long as we stay quiet, nobody will find out."

The brothers were about to leave when something whizzed over their heads. A split second later, they heard a gunshot. They looked toward the far side of the field. Tony Harrison was aiming his rifle directly at them. There was a flash of fire from the barrel, another whizzing over their heads, and then the sound of the gunshot. Barkley was running across the field and howling loudly.

"You worthless poachers!" the angry farmer yelled. "Get the hell off my land, or I'll shoot both of you! Drop those guns, or I swear I'll empty this rifle into both of you!" Tony walked toward them, still aiming carefully.

Butch and Bobby realized the farmer was deadly serious, so they turned and ran toward the tree line. But they didn't drop their guns.

Barkley was fast approaching, still howling.

Solomon had to think fast. The dog would smell him soon and forget about the two men. Summoning up all his courage, the red fox jumped out of the furrow and ran toward the tree line, hopping from mound to mound. He was coming up fast on the dead deer.

Tony had gone out before church to look for the fox and was startled to see Solomon running across the field. He had not expected to encounter the varmint so soon. He quickly turned his sights on the chicken thief and fired several rounds in rapid succession just as Solomon made a mighty lengthwise leap across the fallen deer, flying over the nose, past the white tail, and landing in the plowed dirt beyond, raising a huge cloud of damp dust.

He ran for his life toward another part of the tree line, two or three hundred feet from where the two men had fled.

"Damnation!" the angry farmer yelled at Solomon. "You can jump, you sorry rascal, but, sooner or later, I'm going to shoot you dead, even if you're jumping clear over my barn!"

As Solomon had predicted, when Barkley saw him running and Farmer Harrison shooting at him instead of at the men, the old hound changed directions and began running after Solomon, forgetting the poachers.

The sight of the two men, the dead deer, and the thieving fox all at one time had stunned Farmer Harrison. He quieted down for a moment and stood in his tracks. Then he lowered his rifle and muttered out loud. "Two poaching trespassers and a chicken thief. I should have brought more ammunition."

He began yelling. "Barkley! Come here!"

But the hound kept chasing the fox and disappeared into the woods after his prey.

Tony slowed down and lowered his rifle by his side. He walked up to the deer and stood looking at it, shaking his head. "Thieving rogues," he said softly. "But that fox. I can't believe how far he jumped." He walked toward the tree line after the two men.

Solomon didn't dare look around until he was sure Barkley's howling was growing fainter. When the barking suddenly ceased, he stopped on a small hillock and sat down, panting. He looked back at the woods. He spotted Barkley in the distance, wandering around and sniffing at the ground. After a few minutes, he heard the faint voice of Farmer Harrison yelling again.

"Barkley! Come here, dog!"

Barkley stopped his searching and loped off toward the voice. From somewhere in the woods, Solomon heard several voices yelling at each other, and a moment later there was a gunshot, then several more in rapid succession. A flurry of gunshots erupted for several seconds and stopped abruptly. The unmistakable howling of Barkley came through the tree line.

Solomon sat still; only his tail brushed back and forth on the grass behind him. He had caught his breath and pondered whether to try and return to the chicken coop or head in the other direction. He finally decided to try a second raid on the plump, juicy chickens. But he cautioned himself. *Careful, old fox.*

He stood up and walked briskly to the tree line, constantly turning his head to watch for danger. Peering intently from behind a tree toward Barkley's mournful barking, Solomon could see the dog standing beside the still body of Farmer Harrison lying on the ground. The fox was startled and thought, *What in the world? Is the man dead?*

Shocked, Solomon crept from tree to tree to get a closer look at what had happened.

Barkley was focused on the plight of his master and wasn't paying attention to the fox's movements. When Solomon got to within twenty yards of the scene, he could see Farmer Harrison more clearly. The man was face down on the ground, and a pool of blood had seeped from under his chest and spread around him.

Barkley realized he needed to get help, so he loped off toward the farmhouse, baying loudly through the drizzling rain.

Solomon instinctively knew where the dog was going. He braced himself and crept over to the still body on the ground. Was Farmer

Harrison really dead? It seemed the man was barely breathing. The fox was stunned.

What happened here? Did the two men do this?

Solomon had seen the men many times before during his own hunting expeditions. They were from a farm several miles away. Once, Solomon had even snatched a large tom turkey from their yard. He remembered the men had shot at him, buckshot barely missing his backside as he ran for his life. The men's dogs had given chase, but, like Barkley, they were overweight and slow.

Solomon began conniving. If Barkley returned, Solomon would be able to raid the chicken coop without any trouble. He crept back into the woods and waited behind a large sweet gum tree.

Sure enough, in a short while, he could hear Barkley's faint howling off in the distance. The dog was loping in front of the farmer's wife, who was moving as fast as she could through the soft plowed earth. When they were in the middle of the open field, Solomon began making a wide circle around them, hidden by the trees and heading for the hens.

9

Clara had risen early to finish wrapping all the food in the kitchen. Tony was already up and dressed when she went into the kitchen. He swallowed a last gulp of coffee and left with his rifle, saying he was going to look for the fox.

Clara was still in her housecoat with an apron around her waist and wearing bedroom slippers when she heard gunshots in the distance.

Good! Maybe Tony shot that fox after all, she thought.

In a few minutes, she heard Barkley's howling in the distance. It was getting louder as it approached the house.

When Barkley reached the back porch, she knew something was wrong. This was no ordinary barking. The old hound was frantic. There was no time to get dressed. Barkley wanted her to follow him immediately.

Her heart thumped a little faster as she came down the steps. "All right, Barkley. What's the matter?"

The dog knew what she meant. He turned around and started off toward the field, looking back to make sure Clara was following him. He began loping a little faster and had to stop now and then to make sure she was still behind him.

They got to the edge of the field, and Clara slowed down. Through the light rain, she could see a form lying on the ground in the middle of the field. Barkley ran past it to another form on the far side of the field, and her heart pounded faster as she ran through the plowed furrows. She passed the deer and kept running after the dog.

What in the world happened out here? she thought.

When Clara neared her husband, she let out a scream and ran to him. He was still lying on his stomach. She knelt on her knees and gently put both hands on his head. She felt his neck and put her ear next to his face. She could hear him breathing.

"My God, Tony! What happened?"

Through half-closed eyes, he looked up at her and whispered, "I've been shot, Clara. Get help." Then he passed out.

With much effort, she managed to turn him over on his back and gasped when she saw the blood-soaked bullet hole through his flannel shirt, just below the left shoulder. She removed her apron and pressed it tight against the wound.

She looked at his closed eyes and asked, "I don't know if you can hear me. We've got to stop the bleeding. Can you hold this with your other arm?"

She took his right hand and put it on the apron.

"Press as hard as you can to stop the blood. I've got to call for help before you bleed to death."

She felt his fingers move. He lifted his head slightly and gave a barely perceptible nod. She stroked his gray hair for a moment. Then, moving quickly, she took off her housecoat and wrapped it into a makeshift pillow and gently laid his head on it. He was in shock, and she knew he needed immediate attention.

She got to her feet and looked down at him. "Hang on, sweetheart. Just hang on a little bit longer."

She turned toward the farmhouse, took a deep breath, and ran as best she could over the soft earth to call for help. The thought came to her, *Who in the world would hurt my husband? And why?*

She glanced back and saw that Barkley was on the ground and had put his head on his master's chest.

— ⁓

Meanwhile, Solomon had reached the chicken coop and had run straight inside. Almost immediately, the loud squawking and flapping of panicked hens swirled around him. The dust in his eyes and wings beating against his head slowed him somewhat. Squinting hard, he jumped in the air and caught one of the birds in his jaws. He turned quickly and ran out the door. This time, there was no Barkley and no Farmer Harrison to stop him, so he sauntered leisurely back the way he came.

Coming out of the woods into the plowed field, he saw the farmer's wife trying to run across the plowed furrows in his direction. He made a wide arc to the right and ran with the chicken clenched tight between his teeth.

Clara plodded along as best she could when she glanced over and saw a fox running across the field in the opposite direction. And yes, that was a chicken in its mouth! Clara remembered again why her husband had gone out early that morning and she felt a rush of anger through her pain. She yelled at the fox, "You sorry rascal! I'll get you if it's the last thing I do!"

The fox disappeared into the woods.

10

The sheriff pulled up to the curb outside the office, got out, and opened the back door of the cruiser.

"OK, Sonny. You know where we're going."

Still handcuffed, Sonny had no illusions about trying to run. He knew Sheriff Penegar would be more than glad to shoot him in the back of his leg to keep him in custody. He climbed out of the car and walked to the front of the station. The sheriff opened the glass doors and motioned Sonny to enter. Once inside, the sudden coolness of the air conditioning relieved both of them.

Courtney looked up from her paperwork and gave them a wry smile. "Well, hello, Sonny. Come to stay with us awhile?"

Sonny looked down at her and winked. "Courtney, why don't you take a break a little later from all that dull paperwork and sit with me in the cell for a while?"

"You're out of your league with me, Sonny. Bad boys don't make my heart flutter." She returned to her work and didn't give him a second glance.

Sonny made a nonchalant shrug, but his vanity had been pricked. He went through the back doorway with the sheriff and shuffled morosely down the hallway to the jailhouse cells. Johnston County was up-to-date—each cell was actually a small room with a bunk, sink, toilet, and a desk. The door was steel, and there was a shatterproof window the inmates could look through onto Main Street.

After locking Sonny up, the sheriff went back in his office to start the tedium of paperwork. He was at his desk for about twenty minutes when he heard the siren of the Johnston County Volunteer Rescue Squad ambulance race by the window. Courtney's phone rang. After a moment, a line on his phone lit up, and Courtney appeared in the doorway.

"Tom, it's Clara Harrison. Somebody shot Tony," she said excitedly.

They both looked at each other in stunned silence.

"He's still alive, lying in his bean field. She couldn't move him. That was the rescue squad on the way out there now."

Tom grabbed the phone. "Clara? It's Tom. What happened?"

Courtney watched with concern as the sheriff listened to the details of the shocking news. When he hung up, she looked at him quizzically.

"He's alive. Clara said it looked worse when she first got to him because he was in shock. He'd been shot in the shoulder and lost some blood. She had to run back to the house and get her cell phone."

Courtney bowed her head and slowly shook it back and forth.

He continued, "She's back in the field with him now, waiting for the rescue squad. She managed to stop the bleeding, and he's breathing normally. She thinks he'll be OK."

Courtney looked up and let out a sigh of relief. "Now who in the world would shoot Tony Harrison?" she asked.

The sheriff shook his head in disgust as he stood up and strapped on his holster belt.

"Hold down the fort, Courtney. This is already starting to be a very busy day. I thought Sunday was supposed to be a day of rest."

He grabbed his clipboard and hurried out the door.

Courtney watched through the front window as Tom got into his cruiser for the second time in less than two hours and headed out of town again, this time with the siren blaring.

She looked across the street and saw Millie at the front window of the diner, wondering what all the excitement was about. They both gestured hello. Millie gave a questioning shrug, and Courtney motioned for her to come over to the station. Millie turned the window sign over to read "Closed," locked the door behind her, and hurried across the street.

Courtney sat down behind her desk. Millie pulled up a chair across from her and asked, "What's all the ruckus about?"

"It's been a busy morning, Millie. Tom had to go out first thing and bring in Sonny Folsom. He's locked up in back right now."

"Again?"

"Yep. For about a half-dozen parole violations."

"I knew it was past time for one of the Folsoms to get their butt in trouble."

"Tom thinks he'll wind up doing a long stretch this time. And for what? Stuff that's just plain stupid and half-baked."

"What was the ambulance all about? Is that where Tom went?"

"Hold on to your chair, Millie. Clara Harrison called and said Tony had been shot."

Millie gasped in disbelief.

Courtney nodded her head vigorously. "Yep. Somebody shot him while he was out in the bean field."

Millie looked horrified and started to speak "Is he..."

"No, he's not dead, thank God. Clara said he would probably be OK."

"Do they know who did it?"

"I don't know. Tom's going out there now."

Courtney sat quietly as Millie slowly shook her head in disbelief.

The phone rang, and Courtney immediately picked up the receiver. "Johnston County Sheriff's Office. This is Deputy Krueger." As she listened, she knotted her brow. She put her hand over the phone and said quietly to Millie "It's the minister." She removed her hand and continued to listen.

After a few moments, she asked, "Jerry, is the child still with you and Emma?"

Millie's ears picked up. Intuition told her who they were talking about. Courtney continued.

"Did she say where she was going or when she'd be back?"

There was a pause.

"Well, Jerry, keep the girl with you until someone here calls you. Tom's out on an investigation right now, and it might be a while before he can come out there." Another pause. "OK, Jerry, thanks for the information."

Courtney hung up and glanced over at Millie. There was a long silence. Courtney had a puzzled look on her face as if she sensed something wasn't quite right.

Millie looked straight at Courtney and blurted out a name. "Allison."

Courtney looked back and asked, "What?"

"The child's name is Allison," Millie said. "She and her mother, Mattie, were in the diner early this morning."

Surprised, Courtney nodded her head and related the telephone conversation with the minister. "Well, this Mattie woman came by the preacher's house an hour or so ago with her little girl. Seems the woman used to live here when she was a kid and knew Jerry and Emma from back then."

Millie sat quietly.

"Well, they talked for a while, and then this Mattie asked Jerry and Emma to watch her little girl for a few hours while she went to see her family. Seems she didn't want any of her kinfolk to know about the child and that she was going to surprise them later when she felt the time was right."

Millie listened with a rising sense of alarm.

"Apparently, Jerry and Emma are the only people in town she knew and trusted enough to watch the little girl. Jerry told her it was OK to leave the child with them. Then, after the woman left, he felt he'd better call the sheriff."

Courtney's puzzled look came back as she thought a moment. "Now, why in the world would Jerry and Emma agree to something like that? Something's not right, Millie. I can feel it. Jerry's not telling me something."

Millie was still looking straight at Courtney and slowly nodded her head in agreement.

Courtney shook her head. "This day is getting stranger and stranger, and church ain't even out yet."

11

The sheriff pulled up beside the ambulance at the edge of the bean field. The medical team was struggling with a stretcher, carrying Tony Harrison across the field and trying not to trip in the soft plowed dirt. Clara walked along, holding Tony's hand, Barkley at her side.

The sheriff ran over and helped with the awkward load to the ambulance. Tony's left shoulder was swathed in bandages, and he was still in shock.

The sheriff looked down at him and said quietly, "Hello, Tony. I know you can't talk right now, but I was told you'll be OK, thank God."

The farmer nodded as the EMS volunteers put him in the back of the ambulance. Clara climbed in beside him while the sheriff stood at the back door.

As they were settling in, the sheriff looked inside and asked Clara, "How did this crazy thing happen?"

"Tom. Thank God you're here. Apparently, he was shot over past that tree line. He was able to walk back into the field before he collapsed. I found him lying on the ground over there. You'll see the blood."

He looked at her quizzically for more answers.

"I don't know anything else right now."

The sheriff responded, "I'm going to stay here for a while and investigate. I'll meet you at the hospital later. Maybe we can talk while Tony sleeps, OK?"

Clara nodded silently as the doors were shut.

The sheriff watched as the vehicle left and drove out of sight. He looked around the field and the surrounding woods for a few minutes. He motioned to Barkley and said, "Come on, mutt. Help me pick up the pieces."

With the dog beside him, he walked over to the blood-soaked spot and looked first at the blood, and again at the surrounding area. He pulled his two-way radio out of its holster and radioed the office. "Courtney? It's me. I'm out in the field where Tony was shot. I'm going to look around a bit."

"How is Tony? Is he hurt bad? Where is he?"

"He seems to be all right. He was shot in the left shoulder and lost a lot of blood. EMS took him and Clara to the hospital. Doc Corry is meeting them."

"What happened? Who shot him?"

"I don't know yet. I don't even know if *he* knows. After he's settled in at the hospital, I'm going to talk with Clara."

"OK. Some folks have already started calling in, wanting to know what happened out that way."

"Tell them it's still under investigation, and you can't discuss it at this time."

"All right. I'll see you when you get back. Everything else seems quiet right now. But something interesting happened. You'll need to talk with Millie and the preacher when you get back in town."

Puzzled and exasperated, he asked, "What else has happened?"

"Well, a woman came to town today. Her name is Mattie Folsom. Remember her?"

He wrinkled his brow in thought. "Wasn't she the little girl whose mother married Axel after Maxine Folsom died?"

"Yes, that's the same one. She had a little girl with her."

"Yeah, I remember her. I haven't thought about her in years. She ran away from home about ten or twelve years ago. What about her?"

"Well, like I said, talk with the preacher and Millie when you get a chance. They're the ones who talked with her after she came into town this morning. I never saw her."

Resigned that he wasn't going to get anything more, he said, "OK, Courtney. I'll talk with both of them later."

He put the radio away and began looking around the field. Barkley was still standing by quietly. Drops of blood led back into the tree line, and he followed them. The trail stopped about twenty yards into the woods.

The overhead foliage protected them from most of the rainfall.

"Well, Barkley, this must be where he got shot."

He looked around more intently, walking carefully in an ever-widening circle while searching for evidence or clues. He said aloud to the dog, "I don't see any shells or anything..."

Barkley interrupted him by growling. He looked in the direction of the dog's stare and carefully drew his gun out of the holster. He moved forward cautiously and jumped when he saw a young woman sitting on the ground about thirty yards away, her back against a tall pine tree. She was just watching him. Tom was so rattled that all he could do was stare in disbelief for a few moments. He held the gun up with both hands and pointed it straight at her.

"Who are you?" he yelled.

She didn't say anything.

He told Barkley to be quiet, and they both walked slowly over to her. "Don't move. I'm coming over to talk to you." He kept the gun aimed on her as he moved.

The woman just sat quietly and watched him approach.

Barkley ran ahead and sniffed at her. He backed off and gave a few halfhearted barks that were meant to say, *Well, I'm confused. She seems harmless, but I'd better stand here and guard her just in case.*

The sheriff approached carefully. He stopped about five feet away and looked keenly at the woman.

She was staring up at him with a mixture of defiance and fear. She had been crying and was dabbing her eyes with a bandana. She was young and pretty and wore a tank top, a pair of tight-fitting jeans, and black cowboy boots. Her legs were pulled up to her chest, and her hands were wrapped around her knees. On the ground in front of her was a small revolver.

He stared at it for a moment and looked her in the eyes. "Who are you?"

"Is Mr. Harrison all right?"

He stared again for a moment, and then said, "Well, he's lost a lot of blood, but he'll probably be OK. Who are you?"

She stared off into the distance. Through new tears and softly shaking her head, she said, "I shot the wrong person. I didn't mean to, but I shot the wrong person. At least I think I did."

Pointing at the gun, he asked, "Is this what you think you shot him with?"

She looked up through bleak eyes and nodded. Then she continued crying quietly.

He pulled out his pocket handkerchief and used it to pick up the handgun. He opened the cylinder and emptied the bullets into his hand. One shell had been fired. He put the bullets into his shirt pocket, and, after carefully wrapping the gun in the cloth, he slipped it into his trouser pocket.

"Well, miss, whatever your name is, I'm arresting you for attempted murder. Stand up, and place your hands behind your back. Please don't make any other moves. I don't think I'm going to have any trouble from you, but do exactly like I tell you."

The woman nodded again as she stood up, turned around, and placed her hands behind her.

The sheriff sighed. He regretted having to handcuff this wisp of a woman. He sensed that she was now harmless and wouldn't put up any fight or try to escape. He wasn't even sure if she was guilty of anything. But he was a lawman through and through. He put the cuffs on her gently. "That isn't too tight, is it? It's only until we get to the station."

"It's OK. I know you have to do this, Sheriff Penegar."

Startled at the mention of his name, he carefully turned her toward him and looked into her face. Deep in there somewhere he recognized the young girl who had run away from the Folsoms all those years ago. "Mattie? Mattie Folsom?" He was stunned.

"Yes, it's me, Sheriff. But please don't call me Folsom. I haven't used that name since I ran away."

Still holding her by the shoulders, he stared some more. "Mattie, you've got to tell me everything that happened here, starting now while we drive to town."

She nodded slowly. She seemed to want to tell somebody her story but was ashamed. The sheriff also sensed she was ashamed of more than just shooting Tony Harrison.

Well, he thought to himself, *the Folsom family has been busy as beavers today.* He took her by the arm and led her to the cruiser, being careful to keep her comfortable and not let her stumble in the soft earth.

When he opened the rear door, he said, "I'm not supposed to do this." He reached for his keys and unlocked the cuffs. "The book says I'm supposed to keep you handcuffed until you're safely locked up. But I really don't think you're going to give me any trouble on the way back to town, so I'm taking these off. It's not easy to ride in the back seat with your hands tied behind you. Don't make me have to put them back on, OK?"

She gave him a grateful look and sat down on the back seat and buckled herself in.

As he got in the front, Tom looked over at the dog and said, "Go on home, Barkley, and guard the old mansion."

With that, the sheriff of Johnston County drove his second prisoner of the day to the county jail.

— ⁓ —

Solomon trotted across the countryside with the limp chicken between his jaws, pausing now and then to glance around and make sure he was safe. Although happy with the morning's catch, the sight of Farmer

Harrison lying in the field disturbed him. Solomon never thought of the farmer or Barkley the guard dog as enemies. He was a fox, and it was in his nature to plot and connive and outwit his adversaries. He reveled in his own cleverness and cunning. Whereas most humans would take offense at being called "sly," Solomon would consider the word a wonderful compliment if he could understand English. He got what he wanted by applying this great talent everywhere he went, especially during the hunt. He was a carnivore, and the scent of the hunt and the delicious taste of blood were ever on his mind.

Farmer Harrison had always been sport for him, not an object of fear and hatred. Stealing chickens from right under the nose of that slow old hound Barkley was thrilling. Solomon was energized whenever he successfully stole a day's meal. Today's catch had been too easy though. The real excitement had come earlier during the gunfire in the bean field.

He held his snout high with pride and continued homeward with his catch firmly between his gleaming teeth.

12

*I*n spite of the rain, Main Street in Branton City had filled up rapidly with the festival crowd by the time the sheriff got back to the station. He had to inch his way through the people in order to park in front of the station.

Millie had gone back to the diner to serve breakfast to a couple of local steel workers, but she had been keeping an eye out for the sheriff's return. She had a hunch about who would be with him. When the cruiser pulled up to the curb, she quickly took off her apron and told the two men, "You guys help yourself to anything you want but the cash register. I'll be right back."

With that, she grabbed an umbrella from behind the counter and bolted out the door. She jostled her way through the throng to the front of the station.

Curious, the two customers, Gary and Curtis, looked out the window across the street. Gary was eating a piece of jellied toast; Curtis was finishing off a powdered doughnut. They shrugged at each other.

Turning back to the counter, Curtis said, "Well, let's have some more coffee. And yes indeed, I do believe I'll have another of these fine doughnuts."

"All right. Easy now. Let's be good guests for Millie and not overdo it. In the meantime, while you're at it, bring me one of those honey buns at the end of the counter?"

The two men enjoyed a bigger breakfast than they had first planned.

The sheriff opened the back door, and Mattie got out cautiously, a look of fright and embarrassment on her face. When she saw Millie crossing the street toward them, she bowed her head slightly.

Courtney glanced back and forth from Mattie to the sheriff, not yet knowing what to ask.

Millie reached the little group, and Courtney looked over at her. Sheltered under her umbrella, Millie looked sympathetically at Mattie.

The drizzling rain was running down everyone else's faces, so Millie maneuvered the umbrella as best she could to try to cover the other three.

The sheriff was holding his clipboard along with something wrapped in a handkerchief. He looked at all three women and said, "Well, who knows who here?"

Courtney just looked at him and shrugged.

Millie continued to look at Mattie and said, "I know Mattie. I've known her since she was a little girl. She couldn't have done anything wrong, could she?" The question was almost pleading.

"Well, we're going inside out of the rain and away from the festival crowd. Courtney is going to help me while I interview Mattie. We may get to the bottom of this today, but I don't know." He opened the front door and motioned for Mattie to step inside.

Courtney looked at Millie. "I'll let you know what happened a little later."

The sheriff gave Courtney a stern look, and she quickly added, "I mean, well, just as soon as Tom says I can." She went inside and sat at her desk.

Millie stood still for a few moments and watched through the doorway as the sheriff told Mattie to sit in a chair beside the desk. He laid the handkerchief in front of Courtney and opened it to reveal the revolver.

Millie could barely hear his words, but they still shocked her. "I found this beside Mattie. It's unloaded. Lock it in the safe."

He patted his shirt pocket. "I've got the bullets with me. One of them has been fired. Hand me a plastic baggie."

Courtney reached in a side drawer and gave him one.

He opened it, dropped the bullets in, and sealed it closed. "Put these in the safe too."

He noticed Millie still standing outside the glass door looking in and gave her a grim look. She turned and made her way back across the street to the diner.

Curtis and Gary were still eating when she walked in and went behind the counter.

"Well, guys, need anything else?"

"Nope. Millie, you are one fine hostess," said Curtis.

"Yep. No doubt about it," Gary chimed in. "What happened across the street that you were so fired up about?"

"Someone shot Tony Harrison this morning. It might have been someone I knew a long time ago."

Both men were stunned and spoke at once. "Shot Tony Harrison?" and "Tony's been shot?" and "Is he dead?" and "What's going on, Millie?"

The questions were all jumbled together, but Millie understood. "He's still alive—that's all I know for sure right now. And Clara seems to think he'll pull through. He's in the hospital with Doc Corry."

Curtis asked "Who was that young woman Tom brought back? I've never seen her before, at least not that I recognize."

Millie walked over to the window and gazed across the street at the station. The rain was getting heavier. She said quietly, "She used to live here a long time ago. That's all I know." Millie kept her back to the men and remained silent.

They both realized she was deep in some kind of troubled thought and left her in peace. Anyway, they knew they would pick up the story soon enough.

Curtis put a ten-dollar bill on the counter.

Gary did the same and said "Millie, here's twenty for everything. That should cover the tab."

As they were walking out, she turned, tears running down her cheeks, and said, "You boys don't have to do that. The whole darned breakfast wasn't but eight bucks."

Curtis said "Treat us on the house next time."

She nodded in grateful appreciation as they walked outside and down the street. When they were out of sight, Millie sat down at a table and continued to cry softly.

13

Back at the Folsom estate, the house looked deserted from the front yard, but inside, tensions were high.

Butch had a grim look on his face as he paced around the front room, peeking through the dingy curtains every time he passed a window.

"God Almighty, Bobby. I mean, where the heck did she come from?"

Bobby was sitting on the edge of the sofa, slowly kneading his hands together and looking at nothing in particular. He leaned forward. "I didn't recognize her until she yelled her name."

"Ol' Man Harrison got hit. Was it you?" Butch hoped his brother would say yes and relieve some of the fear that had consumed him.

"I don't know, Butch. It could have been you. We were all shooting at each other after Mattie fired the first shot. It might have been her."

"No. I kept my eye on Mattie. She didn't even know Tony was around. She was dead set on shooting both of us. Jeez, Bobby, what if we killed Ol' Man Harrison?" Butch had talked himself into a state of near-terror.

"Maybe not. I looked back while we were running. Mattie was helping him get out of the tree line. He broke away from her and staggered into the bean field."

Bobby continued to knead his hands together while he thought about the total picture. In some odd way, Butch's fear seemed to calm him down. "Look. If he lives, we're not going to the gas chamber. But we're sure going back to prison. This time for a good long while."

Butch stopped pacing and looked at his brother with angry despair. "Jail?"

"Of course we'll go to jail. What the hell else do you *think* they'll do to us?"

Butch resumed his nervous pacing and said, "Well, suppose it *was* Mattie who shot him?"

"Well, suppose it was. So what? We were trespassing. We were poaching. We killed a doe. Suppose we broke other laws we weren't even aware of. Suppose my butt."

There was a long silence while both men contemplated the possible consequences of the morning's events.

Once again, Butch stopped pacing and leaned against a window, chewing a thumbnail and staring into space. "I'm not going back to jail again, that's for sure. You saw the sheriff this morning. He would have shot Sonny Ray for sure if Sonny hadn't gone peaceably," said Butch. "I never thought she'd come back. I never thought we'd ever see her again."

"She's come back for blood, that's for sure. We damn well better watch out for her," Bobby replied.

Butch pulled away from the window. Talking had calmed him down, and he seemed to fill with a newfound resolve. He got his shotgun from a corner of the room. "I'm going out to look around the place."

Bobby got up from the sofa and stretched. "I'll hunt out back and around the barn. You look out front and around the stable." He got his rifle, tucked a Smith & Wesson revolver in his belt for good measure, and followed Butch out the door.

— ⁓

Inside the station, the sheriff directed Mattie to sit in the front office with Courtney while he made some phone calls. He shut the office door behind him and left the two young women alone together.

Mattie didn't say anything. She just stared at the floor. Courtney looked at her quizzically for a few moments and thought, *What's going on here? Is she a suspect, a prisoner, a witness, or what? Do I need to make sure my gun is handy?*

She realized that Tom was a grizzled veteran and would not have left a dangerous person alone with her, so she relaxed and broke the silence. "I guess I better open a file and start some paper work."

She typed some commands, and a new incident worksheet popped up on the monitor. "Your name is Mattie, right?"

A moment went by before the young woman answered in a soft voice. "Yes. Mattie Hathaway."

"Where do you live?"

"Santa Carla, California."

"Uh...what's the address, Mattie?"

Mattie sensed Courtney was simply trying to do her job as gently as possible. She appreciated the gesture and volunteered all the dry details of her current life as the deputy filled out the worksheet.

Alone in his office, the sheriff stood at the window, staring across the street at the diner. He knew there was a lot more to the young woman's story than she would tell him. He also sensed that it had nothing to do with hiding from the law but hiding from a terrible secret that only another woman might understand. He put on his hat and walked over to the diner. The hat gave him a little cover from the rain.

Millie had stopped crying and was seated at the counter drinking coffee. He sat down beside her without saying anything.

She sighed and asked, "Well? Can I fix you some lunch?"

"Millie, I'm here to find out what's behind all this. You know a whole lot more, and I want to find out what it is."

She said, "Do you want some coffee?"

"Yeah. That would be good right now," he responded. "I haven't had time to finish my first cup this morning."

She got up, moved around the counter, poured a cup, and set it in front on him. Then she sat beside him again.

He took a sip and looked across the counter at the big mirror on the wall. "Why did Mattie try to shoot her brothers?"

"They aren't her real brothers. They're her stepbrothers."

"I know all that. I know Axel wasn't her real father, and I remember that her mother's name was Loretta or Lorraine or something like that. I know Mattie ran away from home years ago."

"It was Lurene. Her mother's name was Lurene," Millie said. She took a sip of coffee and repeated some of the things Mattie had told her. When she finished, she looked out the front window with a solemn look.

The sheriff knew there was more. "OK, Millie. You've told me the outside of this story, but it's all stuff I've known for years. Hell, I've been sheriff around here since those Folsom boys were little kids. And I know some of the bad gossip that surfaced about the time little Mattie ran away. I want to know the *whole* story—why she ran away. I want you to tell me everything you know about the inside of this mess."

She looked at him with a mixture of sadness and guilt. "Well, it's a lot messier on the inside, that's for sure."

"Let's hear it."

With a deep sigh, Millie said, "When Maxine Folsom died and left Axel with those three unruly boys, he looked around for someone to take her place. Axel had never been one to marry for love. He just wanted a glorified housekeeper to help out when he got too drunk to manage things. I doubt if he ever loved Maxine, but she's the only person I knew who could scare him." She took a sip of coffee.

Tom gave her a skeptical look.

She looked back with a wry smile and said, "I saw Maxine giving Axel pure hell several times when they came to town. One time, right here in the diner during lunch, she hit him in the head with a rolled-up newspaper. The place was packed with people. She kept whacking him. He held his arms around his head and ran out the door, with her chasing and swatting him all the way out to his truck, cursing like a sailor. The whole lunch crowd bunched up around the front window, watching the spectacle and laughing their butts off."

They both burst out laughing.

"It's God's truth, so help me. I have no idea what she was so angry about."

He was laughing so hard he had tears in his eyes.

Millie continued. "Maxine sure wasn't afraid of Axel, and that's a fact."

The sheriff finally quit laughing, and they sat in silence. After a bit, he asked, "When did Mattie and her mother come into the picture?"

Millie got up from the counter and went to the window. She stood silently and looked out in space for a while.

He sensed she was thinking hard about what to tell him.

She said "The rain's getting heavier. A storm's coming in from the north. The clouds are as black as the ace of spades." A distant clap of thunder punctuated the words.

After a few moments, she turned and sat down again. "The first time I met Mattie was when she was about six years old. She came to town with her mother every now and then. As I said, her mother's name was Lurene, and she was very pretty, but you had to look hard to see it."

"Where did Axel meet her?"

Millie shook her head and said, "I know you won't believe this, but they met in a church."

The sheriff replied "You're right. I don't believe it."

Millie continued, "Well, apparently one of Axel's drinking buddies told him about a widow woman with a little girl over in Weston County. It seems the woman's husband had been killed in a car wreck, and life got hard real quick for the woman and the child. She managed to get a part-time job at one of the local churches helping in the office.

"Axel's buddy did odd jobs around the church and knew the woman. Axel persuaded his friend to take him along the next time he did some work."

The sheriff nodded slowly, getting the picture, and said, "So Axel accidentally on purpose meets this woman and pours on the smarm."

"Right," Millie answered. "Apparently, the woman fell for it and started dating Axel, if you could call going to the dam in Axel's pickup truck and watching him drink a six pack a real date."

The sheriff shook his head slowly. "The poor woman must have been really desperate to take up with Axel Folsom."

Millie replied, "No, I don't think she was desperate. I think she just needed a man to love and be near her again. And she was so blinded by that need that she thought Axel wanted to love her and be near her in return."

The sheriff sighed. "So, she marries Axel, moves in with him and the three boys, and brings along little Mattie."

Millie nodded.

The sheriff took a sip of coffee. "Didn't Lurene have a family she could turn to? Didn't her deceased husband have a family? Wasn't there anyone anywhere she could have gone to for help?"

Millie shook her head. "All gone. Lurene had no one."

The two sat in silence again. The sheriff stayed deep in thought for a while, barely nodding at no one in particular.

He wasn't looking at Millie when he finally spoke, and his words sliced through her like a knife. "Let's cut to the chase, Millie. When did Axel and the boys start abusing little Mattie?"

14

Solomon made it back to the den with the plump chicken. Once again the little family had a fine meal together. Afterward, all four of them tussled with one another on the sandy shore of the creek bank.

The creek itself was a small tributary of the great Apple River that flowed through the middle of Branton City.

On his recent comings and goings, Solomon's instincts told him the river was rising a little each day. Although he had no way of knowing it, the water's rise was due to the prolonged spring rains that were flooding the smaller rivers that fed into the Apple several hundred miles further north.

Solomon and the missus decided to rest a bit and moved up to the top of the creek bank. They crouched in the grass overlooking the water and watched the two pups, who continued to frolic on the sand below.

It was apparent that the time was ripe for the pups to go with their parents when they went on hunting expeditions. Then the whole family could stay together.

Solomon thought about taking all of them with him the next time he raided the chicken coop. Naturally, he would be the only one to go into the coop. He wanted the missus to stay at a distance with the pups. That way, they could safely observe what being a clever fox was all about.

It was raining harder now, and thunder could be heard in the distance. Some of the heavy rains from up north had reached Johnston County. The two adults beckoned the pups, and they all ran into the comfort of the cozy den.

～ ～

The Apple River was the main artery and life-support system for farmers and industries in the countryside along its lengthy course through five states. From its origins in a mountain range four hundred miles north, the river quickly became a tumultuous thundering of rapids pouring down over rocks until it passed through the gentler slopes of the foothills below. There it gradually slowed to an almost lazy meandering over the lands in its path leading to the sea.

Countless generations had fished, swam, boated, hunted, and traded in and around the Apple River. Since prehistoric times, it was more or less accepted as a silent and benign giant, offering a wealth of various and sundry gifts to those who took advantage of its many treasures.

It had been over a hundred years since the Apple River had flooded enough to cause massive destruction. No one alive in Johnston County had ever experienced the terrible devastation the great river could cause when it got angry.

In the foothills of the Sonoma Mountain Range, about ten miles north of Solomon's den and Branton City, was the Cherokee Dam. It had been built in the 1930s during the depths of the Great Depression as part of the government's Tennessee Valley Authority to stimulate the economy. The vast Cherokee Lake it created covered over forty square miles. Holding back close to three trillion gallons of water, it was the largest dam in the three states that its mighty turbines partially powered.

Cherokee Lake was a source of pride for the region. Beautiful homes and retreats had been built along its intricate shoreline, along with small parks and picnic areas complete with numerous launch sites for boats. People loved the lake, and it was busy most of the year.

The construction of the dam had tamed the Apple River, or so it seemed. As the waters from the lake passed through the dam, they spilled into the same path the Apple had followed for millennia. Continuing its interrupted course, the Apple flowed around the eastern side of what was known as the bluff and past Branton City's town limit, where a park had been built on its bank.

The small creek where the Foxlys lived was several miles west of Branton. It was one of several tributaries of the Apple, and its headwaters were located in the foothills of the Sonoma Mountains. The creek emptied into the Apple about one mile southeast of town.

— ⁓

While Solomon and his family snuggled together downriver, maintenance crews were already working at the dam. They had been summoned several days before as a precautionary measure in case the flooding further north became serious. There would certainly be some impact, but there were no indications yet of how big any such impact might be. The crews would keep a close watch on the water levels and continually inspect the structure of the dam.

A team of civil engineers took up temporary residence in the superintendent's offices located on the overlook and were in constant contact with governor's aides at the state capital. The aides, in turn, were in contact with liaison offices of the state National Guard. There was also open communication with the Federal Emergency Management Agency, which was monitoring developments up through the states for the entire length of the river. The engineers' recommendations would be of tremendous importance in case of an emergency.

For right now, all anyone could do was closely watch the level of the lake. When it reached a predetermined critical point, certain floodgates would be opened to relieve the pressure. Because all rivers were prone to overflow from time to time, the gates had been opened at Cherokee Dam on numerous occasions over the years, causing an inevitable rise in the water levels of the Apple River downstream. But these increases had always been well-managed before, with only minor damage to the adjacent farmlands. If the dam actually broke, the forty square miles of water from the lake would destroy several towns and communities in its path as it swept toward the sea.

It was becoming apparent with each passing hour that the water was rising faster than expected, and the possibility of catastrophic flooding seemed increasingly likely as the level rapidly rose toward the critical point. The mood at the dam had turned from mild concern to nervous tension. The governor herself was preparing to fly to the area by helicopter to assess the situation.

— —

The Foxly family had been sound asleep in the den, with everyone curled up snugly against each other, when Solomon and the missus were awakened midafternoon by the barking of Noah and Eli.

Solomon rose and moved to the den entrance. It was pouring rain. The pups were barking at the water from the creek. It had risen to only a few feet below the den opening.

Using their strong jaws and teeth, Solomon and the missus picked up the pups by the scruffs of their necks and scurried up to the top of the creek bank. Before reaching higher ground, they were soaked from the heavy downpour.

They set the pups in the grass, and then all four of them looked back at the churning waters. The pups began yelping again as a long black water moccasin slithered from the bank into the creek. The family watched cautiously as the snake wriggled downstream in the fast-moving current.

After a few moments, Solomon led the way as the family trotted off into the forest. He wasn't yet sure where they would go, but he knew the den would become a deadly trap.

Several hundred feet into the woods, the family stopped and looked around. There was a lot of activity, as many other animals were running away from the creek too. At any other time, Solomon would have chased one of the rabbits or squirrels, but everyone's minds were on staying alive and escaping the water. Food would have to come later and at a safer distance.

Solomon thought about the chicken coop and decided it would be as good a day as any to carry out his plans to take the pups along with him on his next raid.

And so, the Foxly family set out on what would become their greatest adventure.

15

Soaking wet from the rain, Butch yelled, "Bobby, there's nobody around here right now." He had just made a circuit of the backyard and the barn. Moving around with something to do quieted his fears somewhat. He ran up onto the front porch, where his brother was standing.

Bobby was listening to the heavy rain pounding on the tin roof. He was silently watching the highway through the downpour.

Curious, Butch walked over to him and asked, "What are you looking at?"

Bobby continued looking down the highway. "I'm waiting to see if Sheriff Penegar shows up." He gave Butch a solemn glance. "If Ol' Man Harrison is still alive, he's bound to tell the sheriff what happened, if Mattie hasn't already told him. Then it's just a matter of time before he comes out here to lock us up." He nodded. "Yep, Butch, and when he comes this time, he's going to have plenty of help. He'll bring state troopers with him."

Butch's fear gripped his stomach again. "Cripes, Bobby! What are we going to do?"

"I say let's put as much gear and ammo in the Jeep as possible and get out of Johnston County right now. I mean get clean out of the state altogether and head west."

"Where are we going?" Butch was dumbfounded.

"I don't know yet. But we're going to have to steal some cars on the way. Sure as anything there's going to be an alert put out on us."

"What about the farm? What's going to happen? We can't just pull up stakes and hightail it down the road."

"Butch, the stakes have already been pulled up. They were pulled up the minute Tony Harrison caught us red-handed with the deer."

Since the gunfight, Butch had been running on pure fear. He hadn't been able to think clearly. But now he began to comprehend the full implication of their predicament. Whether they ran away or stayed to face the music, the result would be the same—they had lost the farm forever this time.

He took a deep breath, and his fear gave way to glum resignation. He took another deep breath and ran inside. "Get the Jeep, Bobby! I'll grab what I can!"

16

When Millie finished relating all she knew about the terrible circumstances of Mattie's childhood with the Folsoms, the sheriff said, "Why didn't anyone do anything? Not one hint of any of this ever came my way until after Mattie ran away."

"Look. Nobody else knew for sure either. There was gossip and rumor, but nobody wanted to get involved."

Tom looked grim. "If I had found out, I don't think I would have locked them up. I probably would have shot all four of them instead of taking them to jail. I might still do that after I talk with Tony Harrison."

Millie could see his outrage. "Tom, calm down. This all happened almost twenty years ago. Mattie's alive. Don't go doing anything rash."

A lawman through and through, he sighed deeply and went to the door into the pouring rain to his cruiser. "I'm going to the hospital to see Tony and Clara before I meet with the mayor at the dam."

Millie's ears picked up, and she yelled after him, "The dam? What's wrong with the dam?"

"Nothing yet, at least not anything that I've been told," he yelled back. "We're all on standby because of a lot of flooding up north."

"Is there a chance the dam could break?"

He got into the cruiser and rolled down the window to answer. "I don't know. They've got a team of engineers holed up there watching and waiting. I've got to go. Thanks for the coffee and the information."

He put the car in gear, but before he drove off, Millie ran over to him. She put both her hands on his and said, "Tom, I..." But she stopped herself. Now was definitely not the right time. She had wanted to tell him that he was welcome to come over to her house some night for dinner. She had wanted to tell him that for a long time. Instead, she removed her hands and said, "Be careful."

She ran back into the diner, closed the door, and turned the sign over to "Closed." Then she sat at the counter and cried some more.

The Foxly family made slow progress through the forest. It wasn't because of the rain. A fox can hunt in any kind of weather. It was because the pups were forever tussling with one another and trying to run off in every direction. Solomon knew they couldn't be acting like that when they finally reached the chicken coop. The missus would probably have to give both of them a good nip on their ears and noses to make them settle down. As if she had read his mind, she ran over to the rollicking pups and did just that. They made a few high-pitched yelps and whines, but then they fell in line behind her and trotted along obediently.

Solomon thought, *Good. Now we can make up for some lost time.*

He trotted along faster but was careful not to go too fast—the pups would be exhausted later and unable to make a fast getaway when the time came. He also planned to stop and let everyone rest just before he raided the coop.

Solomon could not know, of course, that Farmer Harrison's entire family had gathered at the farm to watch over the homestead while Clara attended to Tony at the hospital. She had called all three of her children on the way to the hospital and told them what had happened. She related the story of the thieving fox and how it was responsible for Tony's misfortune.

The family didn't go to the church homecoming, and Clara's large assortment of food was still laid out on the kitchen table and counters for the family to eat.

When the whole clan had assembled at the farm, they gathered in the house and under the carport outside. Clara's oldest son, Monte, took the shotgun and told everyone he was going to hide in the henhouse in case the fox came back.

—— ——

Eventually, the Foxly family made their way to some familiar woods, and, through the rain, Solomon saw the coop in the distance. As they approached, he saw Barkley standing under a carport at the side of the farmhouse, along with some children who were playing with him. Some adults sat on lawn chairs in the screened-in side porch. He had seen Farmer Harrison's family on several occasions before, usually sitting out in the sunshine. Solomon thought, *Hmm. This could be trouble.*

He stopped, and the others gathered around him. The missus motioned for the pups to look ahead. They didn't seem to understand what they were supposed to see and began sniffing the air.

Solomon padded cautiously through the woods, the others close behind. When they got to the edge of the woods, the coop was just ahead in plain sight. Solomon crouched low in the grass. Behind him, the missus did the same, with the pups tight by her side.

No one made a sound. Solomon carefully raised his head and sniffed. The smell of the chickens was strong. To his rear, he heard the faint sound of the others sniffing, too. He said to himself, *Good. The pups are staying quiet.*

Solomon carefully eyed the people under the carport. One of the children, a little girl, had climbed on Barkley's back and was pulling his ears in a futile effort to make him move around under the shelter. The old hound stood patiently while the other children coaxed him to give the girl a ride. The adults were talking and laughing among themselves.

The time was perfect. Solomon glanced back at his family and then ran toward the coop, his paws splashing up water. Several yards from the coop, he made a tremendous leap through the doorway.

The missus and the pups watched in fascination. They heard the sudden chaos of sounds as the chickens panicked.

Solomon quickly reappeared, leaping far and high from out of the doorway. But he didn't have a chicken in his jaws. Instead, he barked loudly at his family in a tone that meant for them to flee into the woods. There was a terrific blast from inside the coop, and the sound of buckshot could be heard whizzing through the air over Solomon's head. A large man appeared in the doorway holding a shotgun. He took aim at the fleeing fox and pulled the trigger. There was another blast. Solomon felt a sharp pain in his left ear and front leg, but he was running on pure adrenalin and didn't slow down. The missus and the pups were running back into the forest as fast as they could as he caught up with them.

Barkley heard the first blast and took off running toward the coop. The little girl on his back was suddenly thrown off and began crying when she hit the ground. The adults on the porch stood up and looked toward the coop and caught a glimpse of a fox running rapidly through the grass toward the woods.

Solomon and the family ran together until he knew it was safe once more and stopped to address his wounds. They were protected from the heavy rain by a thick canopy of leaves high overhead. He crouched down on all fours as the missus and the pups looked him over.

The tip of his left ear had been blown off, and his left leg was bleeding. The missus licked his wounds, and the pups started whining, partly in sympathy for their dad and partly in fear. He looked up at them with a forlorn look, and they both licked his face and snout.

After a while, it became clear that his wounds were not life-threatening, and he sat up on his haunches.

Well, he thought, *this lesson could have gone better.*

He wondered where in the world the man with the shotgun had come from. He had been waiting for Solomon, that's for sure.

The more he thought about it though, the more he realized it had been a perfect way for the pups to learn that hunting could be a dangerous business. He knew they would remember what happened and take the experience with them when they finally grew up and went out on their own.

— —

Meanwhile, the man with the shotgun was standing in the doorway of the coop when Barkley ran up to see what happened. By this time, the fox had run deep into the woods, and the old hound wasn't sure which way to go if he gave chase. But to show that he was still vigilant, he loped over to the tree line and sniffed in the air, trying to catch a whiff of the chicken thief. He bayed loudly several times until the man in the doorway called for him. "Stay here and guard the coop, Barkley."

The dog watched as the man walked back through the rain to the farmhouse and joined the people on the porch. The old hound then turned and faced the woods. He sat on his haunches just outside the coop and stood guard, his nose high in the air, sniffing. He let himself get soaking wet as a kind of punishment for failing once again to catch the chicken thief. Finally, he got up and moved to the doorway. The chickens had calmed down and were nesting again. He lay on his side on the wooden floor, and, as he drifted off to sleep, he realized how much better it felt not having small children on his back pulling his long ears.

— —

The Foxly family walked further into the woods and rested under a giant pine tree. The rain was getting heavier, and the pups whined again with hunger. Solomon and the missus licked their faces and tried to calm them down.

Where can we get some food? Solomon thought.

He looked around, nose twitching, ever alert for the slightest smell of something to eat.

Rivulets of water streamed down from the hill behind the pine trees. There was no letup in the rain. Pools of water formed on the ground as the earth became saturated. Solomon knew the family needed to move up the hill. He led the way through the pine forest until they reached the summit and sat to rest. They could see a long way, and black storm clouds spanned the length of the horizon. The lightning and thunder frightened the pups, and they cowered next to their parents.

Suddenly, Solomon's ears pricked up. He heard a high-pitched sound coming from a distance. The missus and the pups also took notice, but none of them knew what it was. Solomon adjusted his ears and reckoned the sound was coming from the direction of the lake. He looked around and saw other animals scattered about listening intently. Something in the distressful sound made his heart race.

A few of the animals moved away from the direction of the siren. Solomon and the missus knew they had to move too. As hungry as they were, the threat of danger was more compelling.

Joining a growing number of other forest creatures, the Foxlys huddled tightly together and trotted away from the mournful noise. Food would have to wait.

17

It was seriously raining when the sheriff arrived at the dam and climbed the spiral staircase to the top of the west tower. He went outside and stood on the widow's walk overlooking the dam. Two hundred feet below, engineers at the base were inspecting the concrete. He called down to Jeb Armstrong, the chief engineer. He had to yell loudly because of the noise from the rain.

The engineer motioned for him to join them. The sheriff made his way down several stairwells and corridors until he was outside again at the base. He looked quizzically at Jeb and the people gathered around him. "What's the story?"

The chief pointed upward. "Look for yourself."

The sheriff stared up at the massive wall, craning his neck uncomfortably because of the height and squinting because raindrops were splattering his face. He couldn't detect anything with his untrained eyes.

The chief pointed to a barely perceptible line running irregularly up the mammoth structure. "See that hairline crack? She wasn't there this morning. And there are about a dozen more along the main wall."

The sheriff looked closer and noticed a thin black line running crookedly up the concrete. There were more to the right and left. "How bad is it?"

"She's not going to hold."

The pronouncement was startling. The hairs on the back of the sheriff's neck stood up, and, for a brief moment, he thought he might wet his pants. "How much time do you think we have?"

"Four, maybe five hours."

The sheriff looked grim. "We've got to get everyone out of town. Did you alert the governor?"

"Yes. The National Guard has been on standby since six o'clock this morning. They're on the way from the staging area in McBee County."

The sheriff took a deep breath. "Well, I guess I'd better set off the alarm system for the whole county."

Another engineer spoke up. "And we'd better get our own butts out of here right now."

Everyone moved quickly toward the metal stairs that led to safety.

The sheriff motioned for the rest of them to climb up ahead of him. He yelled up to no one in particular, "Are the turbines crew and the other work gangs still down in the hole?"

"No," someone shouted, "we sent them all home thirty minutes ago. Everyone's gone."

He made his way back to the top of the tower and pulled the emergency switch that would set off sirens scattered about the county. Then he called Courtney on his walkie-talkie. "Courtney, come in."

"I'm here, Tom."

He could hear the siren in the background.

The mayor, fire chief, and the hospital had been told to keep their radios open and close by. They were patched into the same eliminator code as the sheriff's office, so he could transmit to everyone at once.

"Brad, are you there?" the sheriff asked.

The mayor replied, "Right here."

"Joe? How about you?"

Joe was the fire chief. When he responded, "Yes," the sound of men scurrying about and the roar of the two engine trucks could be heard in the background.

"I'm here, too, Tom." It was Doctor Fraley, chief of staff at the hospital.

"I guess all of you know why the siren went off."

"That bad, huh?" Courtney asked.

"We've got to get as many people out of town as we can. The dam's going to break in about four hours, maybe a little longer if we're lucky."

Because it was situated in the shadow of the large dam, it was mandatory that Johnston County have an emergency evacuation plan. Once every six months for the past forty years, the powers that ran the county had held practice disaster drills. And now, it seemed, all that practice was going to be tested and stretched to the limits.

Branton City had a population of eighteen thousand with another sixteen thousand or so living in the rest of the county. For all those people, the dam had always been a part of the landscape. Most of them rarely, if ever, gave it a second thought. Everyone was aware that it might break one day, but they didn't worry about it. After all, the dam was maintained by competent people who knew what they were doing. The blaring sirens caught everyone by surprise.

The sheriff had a lot on his mind and had to keep thinking fast. Would people panic? Would the roads be jammed? Was looting a serious possibility?

The mayor spoke up. "The National Guard is on the way along with the Red Cross. Helicopters have been ordered to fly in from Shaughnessy Marine Air Base to help get people out of town. But that may take too long. I don't think there's time to wait for outside help. We've got to get everyone moving west of town immediately. Doc Fraley, are you set to evacuate the hospital?"

The doctor cut in. "Well, we have enough buses to take most of the ambulatory patients to safety, and some of the staff are going to help take the rest. But we have about twenty bedridden patients, and it's going to be a squeeze to crowd them into the available ambulances."

The sheriff said, "Joe, I was coming to the hospital anyway to see if I can talk with Tony Harrison. I'll stay there and help evacuate the patients. Courtney? Can you still hear me?"

"I hear you fine, Tom," she cut in.

"Courtney, I should be in town giving you a hand, but I've got to help at the hospital. They're closer to the dam, and we need to get them to safety. You heard what the mayor said about the National Guard and the marines. Maybe they'll get there in time to help, maybe not. Can you handle it on your own?"

Courtney hesitated a moment, and then answered. "Sure."

"Listen. Go in the bottom-right drawer of my desk and grab several of the temporary deputy badges. Deputize some people to help you."

"Should I take along the Bible for swearing in?"

He heard a touch of humor in her voice and knew he could count her to do her job. "No. No need for swearing in. I'm sure there will be enough swearing going on as it is."

Courtney responded with a loud "Hah!"

The mayor spoke up. "We'll send four SUVs from the courthouse. Tom? What about the jail? Do you have anyone dangerous locked up?"

"Well, right now, there are only two prisoners. Sonny Ray Folsom and a young woman who may or may not have shot Tony Harrison."

"Geez, Tom! An incorrigible troublemaker and a possible assassin?"

"I really don't think Sonny Ray is going to cause any mischief. The only thing he might do is skip out of the state altogether to avoid going to trial. And that could be a plus for the whole county. The girl is harmless. I'd be willing to bet my last dime on it."

"Well, don't bet anyone's *life* on it. It's your call."

The sheriff replied, "OK. Courtney, let Sonny Ray and Mattie out of jail. But keep Sonny in your custody until I get back to town."

"Roger that, Tom." she replied.

— —

Inside the station, Courtney shook her head in disbelief as she got up and walked hurriedly into the back. Then the thought hit her. *The river!*

The bridge! She clicked on the handset. "Tom, I've got to check the bridge! Half the crowd is parked on the other side of it!"

"You're right. If it's flooded, you'd better block it off and direct all traffic away from it."

She hurried back to the front of the station to let the two prisoners go.

18

Solomon and the missus trotted awhile with the pups tagging behind. They were still trying to get away from the frightening noise of the siren when they realized the same sound was coming from the town as well as the lake.

They stopped, pricked up their ears, and looked around. All sorts of forest creatures were moving in different directions, apparently as confused as the Foxlys were.

Movement higher up on the hill caught Solomon's eye. The mother bear and her two cubs were lumbering down the hill toward them. He thought, *This could be trouble.*

Sure enough, when the bears came close, Noah and Eli ran over to the cubs and began frisking about with them in harmless play. This did not sit well with their mother, who immediately stormed over, growling. The pups, not realizing they were in grave danger, yipped and gamboled around her. She snarled and charged, grabbed Noah in her mouth, and shook him about. Eli ran to his mother in terror. The bear was ready to kill Noah when Solomon thought, *I've got to get her attention!*

Solomon sprinted over to one of the bear cubs and bit it on its snout hard enough to make it yelp in pain.

The mother bear looked over at her cub, dropped Noah to the ground, and ran at Solomon, madder than ever.

Noah, limping slightly and with some blood on his fur, ran over to his mother, whimpering.

Solomon had just enough time to bark at his family to run as fast as they could away from the area. He watched as they scampered down the hill and out of sight.

The mother bear was so close now that Solomon could see straight into her face. She had the look of protective rage only a parent can have at the sight of an offspring in danger. In a split second, the sly fox would be dinner for the three bears if he didn't act at once.

He let go of the cub's snout just as the mother bear gave him a swat, knocking him to the ground several feet away. Dazed, Solomon jumped to his feet and sprang away, running as fast as he could down the hill but on a different path than the one his family had taken.

The bear was still chasing him all to the bottom of the hill when Solomon suddenly came to a deep ravine about fifteen feet across. The sheer walls were about thirty feet to the bottom on his side and about twenty feet down on the opposite side. At the base was a rocky creek. The walls were too high to fall over without serious injury. He looked back in panic. The bear was closing in fast. *What to do?* Solomon thought.

Then the idea hit him. Like the Scout he had seen the day before, he ran back toward the bear!

The family was watching from a safe distance, and, for a moment, the three of them wondered if he had lost his way or lost his mind.

When Solomon got within several feet of the enraged animal, he suddenly turned around and began running back toward the ravine.

Just as he reached the edge, Solomon gave a mighty leap and jumped clear across the ravine, landing in a puddle on the other side. He got up, ran a few more yards, and then stopped. He turned around and shook the water from his coat.

Sitting down on his haunches, he looked back across at the angry bear on the other side running toward the rim of the ravine. Solomon knew he was safe and that the bear could never make a jump like that.

＊　＊

The bear stopped at the edge, barely able to keep from tumbling into the abyss in front of her. She looked across the expanse at Solomon. He had a smug look on his face, she thought, sitting there on his rear end, staring straight at her. His bushy tail brushed slowly back and forth behind him. He opened his mouth in a wide yawn, exposing those snow-white teeth and fangs in a perfect insult.

The bear cubs caught up with their mother and stood beside her, looking across at what might have been a tasty meal.

＊　＊

From a safe distance, Solomon's family was still watching the event unfold too.

All parties concerned were in awe of the same thing—that fantastic jump the fox had made for his escape.

＊　＊

I did it! thought Solomon.

He finished yawning and ran his tongue all the way around his snout, licking his lips. It was his way of expressing victory.

The bears stood for a few moments, and then the mother turned and lumbered back up the hill in the rain, the cubs trailing behind.

The missus and the pups watched until the bears were out of sight and then came out of hiding. They walked over to the ravine edge and stood looking at Solomon on the other side, waiting for him to make a move.

Solomon realized that he couldn't make the jump back because the side where his family stood now was much higher, and he would never be able to make that kind of leap.

In his comings and goings, Solomon hoped there might be a way across the ravine without jumping.

He walked along the edge, moving upstream. The others instinctively knew to follow his course. The family moved silently along, Solomon on one side of the ravine, the missus and the pups on the other, not really knowing where they were headed.

From time to time, the pups wandered too close to the ravine edge, and both Solomon and the missus barked a warning.

The sirens continued to blare through the pouring rain. All of them sensed something terrible was about to happen, but Solomon kept walking and looking across the chasm to make sure his family was keeping up with him.

Eventually, what looked to be a tree that had fallen across the ravine appeared far ahead. He ran toward it, the missus and the pups running along with him on the other side.

Solomon, being the fastest, reached the tree before the others had a chance to go very far. They watched as Solomon leaped onto the log and raced across to the other side and ran to his family.

They briefly huddled close together in the rainfall, and then moved to a cluster of tall pines for shelter. The high canopy brought some relief from the water coming down.

Solomon looked around and decided they would continue to follow the creek upstream. He stepped out into the rain and led the family back to the bank, where they started moving again on their journey to safety. He remembered that the creek flowed down from the high mountain to the north.

19

On his cell, Sonny Ray was lying on the cot in his underwear, listening to the roaring downpour, when sirens began blaring. He jumped up and looked out the window at Main Street. The sidewalks and the street were clogged with people jostling each other as they tried to get to their cars. Many had parked west of town in the park behind the bandstand. Many more had parked east of town in a large field on the far side of the bridge. Helicopters could be heard flying overhead.

What the hell is going on? he thought.

He was still staring out the window when Courtney appeared and opened the cell door.

"Get dressed and come with me, Sonny. We've got to hurry. The dam's going to break. The National Guard and marines are on the way, but there isn't time to wait for them. You're out of your cell but still in my custody until the sheriff gets here. So stay close by, because I may need your help. And don't worry—I'm not going to let you drown." With a half-smile, she added, "Try to escape, and I'll shoot you."

Good grief! Sonny thought. *All the choices I've been given today involve somebody shooting me!*

Courtney moved to the next cell and opened the door. Mattie was standing at the window.

"Mattie, get out. Run. The dam is going to break. Get out of town."

Mattie didn't seem to be listening. She was in her own world and continued to stare out the window at the downpour.

Sonny hurriedly threw on his shirt and pants, slipped on his shoes, and followed Courtney to the office. "How am I going to get out of town? I don't have my truck."

Courtney opened the front door, and they looked out at the pandemonium breaking loose on the street. A panic was imminent as the crowd tried to move in both directions.

"I've got to check the bridge." She grabbed a bullhorn from the front wall and moved out on the sidewalk. She turned and said, "Millie's going to need a ride too. Go back and get Mattie. She's still in her cell. Then go across the street and get Millie. All three of you jump in the cruiser and take as many people as you can get to fit inside the car."

Sonny looked startled. "Mattie? Mattie who?"

As Courtney ran out of the office, she hollered over her shoulder, "Mattie Hathaway. She's in cell number three, right next to yours."

She threw the cruiser keys to him, then ran down the street toward the bridge.

Sonny had a funny feeling about this Mattie Hathaway. He paused at the entrance to the office and thought about the young girl who had run away so long ago. He hadn't thought about his long-gone stepsister in ages.

Unpleasant thoughts, buried and forgotten for years, surfaced. He remembered how his older brothers deliberately tripped her when she was small and then stood by and grinned when she fell and cried. Sonny wasn't much older than Mattie, and he did his fair share of picking on her.

Later, when Mattie was about ten or eleven, the abuse took a darker turn. Sonny wasn't old enough to understand what Butch and Bobby were doing to the girl and he never participated. He remembered how the older brothers walked out of her room and joined their father in the kitchen. From down the hallway, Sonny heard them laughing. Through the shut door, Sonny heard Mattie whimpering for her mother. He remembered he felt he should at least try to comfort her, but something—fear of his brothers and father, maybe—he didn't understand held him back.

Sonny's thoughts returned to the present. *Why in the world would Mattie come back here?*

Apprehension made him walk to cell number three slower than the emergency called for. Was it really the Mattie he once knew? If so, what was she doing here in Branton City? And why would she be locked up in jail?

He stopped just before he got to Mattie's cell and waited a moment. Then, with a deep breath, he moved to the doorway and looked inside.

Mattie was sitting on the edge of the bed. She looked up at Sonny, and they both stared at each other for a long while.

Sonny vaguely recognized her and noticed she was edging away from him. He also noticed she was a woman now and much prettier than the young girl he had once known.

Her eyes filled with tears, and her face was that of a frightened and cornered little girl. But her voice was filled with quiet rage, and her small hands were clenched in tight fists. "What are you doing here?"

Sonny paused. He had seen that same frightened look on his stepsister when she was too small and vulnerable to defend herself against the large bullies she had been forced to live with. A teardrop trickled down her cheek.

He stood in the doorway and said, "I'm not going to hurt you, Mattie. I swear. I'm not even going to touch you."

"What do you want?" she said, her voice rising.

"We've got to get out of here right now. The dam is going to break and flood all of Branton."

Mattie suddenly realized the danger her young daughter was in and a look of pure terror, bordering on panic, came over her. She jumped up and ran past Sonny to the front office. She looked at Courtney's empty chair and then out the window at the pandemonium in the street.

Sonny followed her and stood at a distance.

She was close to hysterics when she yelled, "Allison! I've got to get Allison!"

Sonny tried to calm her. "Who's Allison?"

"My little girl!" Mattie ran out the door with Sonny close behind. They stood in the street where the noise was so loud that Sonny had to shout.

"Where is she?" Sonny yelled.

But Mattie began running up the street and didn't pay any attention to him.

Sonny stood and watched as she disappeared in the crowd. Then the thought struck him—here was a chance to skip town on his own. He looked around at the people cramming into cars and trucks and people on foot in the street pushing and shoving each other trying to move in both directions.

He watched the turmoil and plotted. Courtney had run down to the bridge and wouldn't see him.

He casually walked across the street and mingled with the crowd moving on the sidewalk.

He walked for a block or two and was about to duck down a side street and be on his way, free as a bird. He glanced across the street but didn't see Mattie anywhere in the crowd.

A young family blocked his way. They were having a difficult time with three young children. The mother was trying to lead her small daughter, but the girl wouldn't move. The father had two older boys in tow. People were moving past and jostling them. The parents had a quick discussion. The father handed the boys over to his wife and hoisted the little girl onto his shoulders as the family began moving again.

Beam me up, Daddy! The thought flashed through Sonny's mind. He moved into a doorway and stood still for a few moments. He watched the family continue walking away, and tears welled up in his eyes as he remembered those long-ago times with his own daughter. That special place in Sonny's heart was still there, and it still ached for those innocent memories he had shared with little Sara.

He thought about Mattie when she was frail and defenseless. No one in the Folsom clan had ever picked her up and carried her around on their shoulders. He thought about what Mattie's daughter might look like. Could she look like Sara? Maybe. A few more tears ran down his cheeks. The thought of running away left him as he realized he had been running his whole life. Even going to prison was a way to run away.

Sonny suddenly felt more alert and alive than he had ever experienced. A warmth spread through him. His usual self-centeredness gave way to a feeling of kinship with the folks of Branton City who surrounded him. For the first time, he saw them—really saw them. They seemed different now. These were the same people he had known and feared his entire life. He had pestered them and fought with them with a sneering cynicism he had been born into. They now appeared to him as the family and friends he had needed from the beginning.

A transformation of character such as Sonny experienced can seem to border on the miraculous, but the kindheartedness that Sonny had begun to feel before he went to prison had grown into his consciousness.

He looked across the street. Mattie was nowhere to be seen. Sonny knew she was probably running by now to get to her daughter, wherever that was.

He moved out of the doorway and maneuvered through the writhing mass of people to a sidewalk bench. He jumped up on the seat and stood on his tiptoes, looking far up the street for any sign of Mattie, but he couldn't see her.

He looked down the street and saw Millie standing outside the door of the diner. She had a shocked look on her face as she watched the crowd trying to move in both directions. He cupped his hands to his mouth and yelled. "Millie!"

She looked over at him.

"The dam's going to break! Get out of town!"

Millie gave him a curious look and thought, *What's happened to Sonny all of a sudden, giving a hoot about others?*

He stepped down from the bench and maneuvered his way over to the diner.

He stood in front of her as she looked at him with suspicion. "You have to get out of town, Millie. I've got to find my stepsister and help her."

He moved to another bench and stood on the seat.

Millie stared at Sonny in amazement. She muttered softly to herself, *I'll be darned! He really wants to help me and Mattie!*

She moved over to the bench and climbed up with him. He looked at her in surprise.

She said, "We'll both find her. Which way did she go?"

Sonny pointed up the street. "She's up there in the crowd somewhere."

They started looking intently for her.

Meanwhile, Courtney reached the bridge and pushed her way to the front of the people who were already there. They all watched as rapidly rising water shipped over the top of the bridge, obscuring the pavement beneath.

No one, especially children and the elderly, would be able to cross safely. Courtney thought, *I've got to get everyone moving the other way!* She held up the bullhorn. "Listen to me! We can all see the bridge is dangerous and can't be crossed. It's going to get worse."

The crowd quieted down somewhat.

"I know your cars are parked over there, but you can see you can't make it. We've got to get everyone moving in the other direction, or we'll all drown. Start moving back toward town, and spread the word to everyone to go west, toward the school. The marine helicopters you hear flying overhead are landing on the campus grounds. They'll fly as many of us out of here as possible. Let me get in front, and I'll keep warning everyone with the bullhorn."

The group calmed down considerably as they listened and sensed she would lead them to safety. She ran quickly up the pathway the crowd opened up for her and started walking back toward the center of town, the folks behind her obediently following.

As they ran into others who were still heading toward the bridge, Courtney continued yelling through the bullhorn, "The bridge is flooded. Go back! You can't reach your cars. Go back! Keep heading west. Head to the school and the helicopters."

The ever-enlarging group following Courtney kept a remarkable semblance of order in what could have been mass panic.

She continued, "Calm down and listen up! You're all doing great. We're going to stick together and help each other survive. Those of you parked near the bandstand, take a few people with you whose cars are stranded across the bridge. Head west, away from the river!"

— —

Sonny and Mille heard Courtney speaking through the bullhorn as the crowd from the bridge approached the center of town. Courtney stopped in front of the police station and motioned for the people to keep moving past her.

Millie yelled, "Courtney! Over here! Look over here!" Her voice was drowned out by the roaring noise.

As Millie yelled, Sonny turned and continued to look for Mattie.

He finally spotted her far up the street, trying to push her way through the crowd. He tapped Millie on the arm and began pointing excitedly. "There she is!"

Millie looked but couldn't see anything.

Sonny reached into his pocket and retrieved the keys to the cruiser. He handed them to Millie. "Here. Courtney wanted us to get people into the cruiser and get out of town. You do it. I'm going to find Mattie."

Millie looked curiously at the keys in her hand.

Sonny turned and looked over at Courtney. He cupped his hands together and began screaming. "Courtney!" He screamed several times until she finally heard and looked over at him. He pointed at Millie standing beside him. "I'm going to help Mattie!"

Courtney yelled, "Where did she go? She was supposed to be with you."

Sonny pointed up the street and yelled, "She ran off to get her daughter. I gave Millie the keys to the cruiser, and she will drive people out of town. I'm going to find Mattie and help her."

Courtney stared dumbfounded as Millie nodded her head in agreement. She then stared even harder as her prisoner stepped off the bench and helped Millie down. Courtney thought, *If he was going to run away, he'd be gone by now.*

She made a split-second decision and nodded her assent at them before they disappeared from view.

Marines in fatigues moved rapidly into the town and helped lead people toward the school.

Sonny and Millie moved a few yards through the throng when he stopped and looked at her. "Millie, you heard what I told Courtney. Stay here and help her. She needs you more than I do. I can help Mattie by myself."

She balked and said, "She won't go with you, Sonny."

"Why not?"

"Why do you think Mattie was in jail?"

Sonny looked at Millie with a frown.

"Somebody shot Tony Harrison this morning. He's still alive. Mattie was there."

"What are you talking about?"

"I don't know what happened out at the Harrisons or how Mattie was involved, but Tom brought her in along with a gun he found on her."

"Why would she want to shoot Tony Harrison?"

"She didn't want to shoot Tony." She looked hard at Sonny. "I believe she came back to Branton to shoot you and Bobby and Butch, but something went wrong."

Sonny sighed. He looked at Millie, and they both knew what had never been mentioned before. "Well, I don't blame her, Millie. All three of us had it coming."

Millie lowered her eyes.

Sonny touched her on the arm. "I can't change the past, but I can at least try to make up for some of it. She needs to get her little girl, and I want to help."

"Allison is the little girl's name." Millie nodded.

"Yes, Allison. Go on. Help Courtney. Drive the cruiser. I have to do this on my own."

He disappeared into the crowd, and Millie made her way over to Courtney.

When he reached the sidewalk, Sonny stood on another bench. He was getting closer. Not far away, Mattie was talking excitedly with the driver of a car that was inching its way through the tangled snarl. The driver was shaking his head and finally rolled up his window to shut her out.

She turned back to the sidewalk with a desperate look on her face.

Sonny cupped his hands to his mouth and yelled. "Mattie!"

Once again he had to yell at the top of his lungs until Mattie finally looked in his direction.

"Mattie! Wait there!"

She just stared at him.

He jumped down from his perch and forced his way through the crowd until he reached her. They stood several feet apart and looked at each other.

"What do you want, Sonny?"

He could feel the bitterness in her words. "I'm going to help you get your little girl."

"I don't need your help."

"There isn't time to argue, Mattie. For the first time in your life, I want you to trust me." Sonny looked in the street at the logjam of vehicles and pedestrians that had brought traffic to a halt and realized they had to get off Main Street in order to keep moving. He gestured with his arm. "We've got to get away from this." He grabbed her hand and began pulling her. She tried to free herself, but he wouldn't let go. "Mattie. Please. Just trust me. I once had a little girl, too. If it had meant her life, I would have let my worst enemy save her."

Reluctantly at first, Mattie let him lead her back toward the jail. She realized that Sonny had been too young to participate in the worst of the abuses she had suffered in the Folsom household.

"What are you doing, Sonny? We're going in the wrong direction."

"No, we're not, Mattie. Watch."

He led her past Alvin's Antiques to the small alleyway that separated it from Furr's Feed Store. "Come on; we can make better time this way."

They ran down the alley and came out on Meadow Avenue, where it wasn't as congested. People were getting into their cars and trucks, and others were running up the sidewalks toward the parking field. The vehicles were moving faster than those bogged down on Main Street.

Sonny and Mattie stopped and looked around. Sonny asked, "Where is she?"

"At Pastor Abernathy's house."

"Jerry and Emma's place?"

Mattie nodded.

"That's about two miles away. Let's see if we can get a lift." He looked up and down the street and spotted Frank Gronsbell driving his pickup. Frank was one of Sonny's barhopping buddies. The truck was loaded down with people.

Sonny ran to the truck with Mattie in tow and asked, "Which way are you going?"

Frank looked impatient and said, "Out Coopersville Road, toward the bluff."

"That goes right past the preacher's house," Sonny responded.

With his thumb, Frank indicated all the people inside the cab and in the bed of the truck. "I'm full up, Sonny."

"Frank, I know you're packed, but I've got to get out to Reverend Abernathy's place. My stepsister's little girl is out there. We can ride on the tailgate if we let it down."

Frank looked quizzically at Sonny, and then at Mattie. "You've got a stepsister?"

"Yes." Sonny turned and looked at Mattie. "I'll explain later." He moved to the back of the truck and lowered the tailgate. "You're going right by the preacher's house."

The people in the bed of the truck were huddled together and using whatever clothing they had to protect themselves from the water pouring down. Some of them knew Sonny and frowned questioningly at each other. No one recognized the young woman.

Sonny briefly acknowledged their stares and nodded. Then he and Mattie hopped on the tailgate. Frank looked back with skepticism and began moving again.

— ⌣

Millie stood beside Courtney in the middle of the street, both of them soaking wet, and held out the keys Sonny had given her. "Here are the keys to the cruiser. Where is it?"

Courtney nodded at the keys and said. "The cruiser is in the parking lot behind the station. Grab some people and take them through the station and out the back door. Go out Meadow Avenue to Coopersville Road, and head west."

They hugged each other.

"OK. I'll come back and get more people if there's still time," Millie said.

They hugged again.

Millie told some people to come with her as she opened the door to the station. They followed her through a series of hallways to the back exit, where a set of wrought-iron steps took them down to the parking lot. She got behind the wheel as eight others crammed their way into the car.

Cramped tight with three people beside her in front and five more in the back, she started the engine and moved onto the street. Traffic was moving steadily to Coopersville Road. Apparently, everyone else had the same destination in mind.

— ⌣

Branton City's two fire trucks had been parked near the bridge for children to play on during the festival. The volunteer firemen cranked them up, and the trucks slowly worked their way up Main Street. Only the drivers stayed in the trucks. The rest of the firemen along with marines walked beside it and helped people find a spot to hang on. The trucks quickly became packed. The sirens were turned on, and folks in the street automatically moved over to let them pass.

Courtney looked around and saw the situation was getting better. The crowd was thinning out as people reached the outskirts of town and dispersed, making their way west as best they could to the school.

She stood in the street until the marines and the firemen had led the last of the stragglers to the far end of town and the waiting helicopters. When she looked back toward the bridge, she saw the flooding had reached the business district. She ran down to the first building and sloshed through the swirling water. It was Branton City Savings and Loan. She opened the front door and yelled through the bullhorn, "Is anyone still in here? Come out now, and get to safety!"

No one answered, and she yelled again to make sure.

Courtney moved quickly and methodically from door to door in this way, zigzagging back and forth through the rain across Main Street to each and every storefront, trying to ensure that the people she had sworn to protect were going to escape the coming disaster.

It took her almost an hour to finally reach the other end of town. She stood by the bandstand with arms akimbo and watched as the remaining cars in the parking lot made their way west.

The last car in the lot pulled over and stopped beside her. Ray Williams got out and opened the passenger door for her. Three other people were in the front seat, and six were packed into the back. Ray made a show of bowing like a chauffeur and said, "It's your turn, Deputy Kruger. We noticed you just a few minutes ago, yelling into Connie's Hair Salon over there. You were making sure the town was empty and folks were safe before you took off, weren't you?"

Courtney nodded shyly in embarrassment.

"If we had known, we would have helped. By the time we saw you, you were right across the street, so we just waited here for you."

Gene Andrews leaned forward in the back and said, "We're all proud of you, Courtney. You are one fine cop. Now it's time to save yourself."

Others in the back commented on her heroics: "Branton's lucky to have you" and "You've got guts, Courtney."

Ray said, "Get in out of the rain, Courtney, and let's get the heck out of Dodge."

Still blushing and at a loss for words, Deputy Sheriff Courtney Kruger edged her way onto the front seat. Ray shut the door and got back in the driver's seat, and the last of Branton City's townsfolk headed for safety.

20

On the northern side of Johnston County, about halfway between Branton City and the Cherokee Dam, a small mountain rose out of the gently rolling hills and flat plains. Its geological name is a monadnock, although few people in the region ever referred to it as such. It was simply called the bluff because of its high cliff overhanging the Apple River on its eastern side. This lone little mountain had been designated a state park and animal refuge. People from near and far came to visit and enjoy its beautiful atmosphere. Its sloping sides were covered with thick underbrush and trees of every description. It had hiking trails and picnic areas, and, at the top, there was a magnificent view of Johnston County and beyond. Branton City's buildings and surrounding farms and homesteads could be clearly seen from the south overlook.

Because it rose several hundred feet higher than Cherokee Lake, anything at its apex would be protected from flooding should the dam break. Solomon knew the family would be safer on high ground.

The headwaters of the creek Solomon had been following were on the western side of the Bluff. A tributary of the Apple River, this creek meandered south from the base for about ten miles below Branton City before joining the Apple.

As the family traveled, it was obvious the creek was rising and would soon overflow its banks. They trotted and then broke into a run when the water began sloshing around their paws.

The rainfall seemed to be getting heavier. The Foxlys were soaking wet when they reached the base of the mountain. They had been moving uphill, but the groundwater was still a threat. They looked up through the forest and knew they needed to get further up the slopes.

Solomon took the lead and began trotting up the mountain. Noah and Eli stayed close behind him, and the missus took up the rear to make sure the pups were safe. There was no letup from the pouring rain.

A few other animals moved along beside them. A family of deer ran past down the hill, apparently in a panic. Solomon knew he must stay calm in order to protect the family, so he kept looking ahead, glancing back now and then to make sure the others were still in tow.

They came near a hiking trail and saw a family of humans wending its way up to the top. Several children spotted the foxes and pointed excitedly. Their parents looked over at Solomon and simply smiled. There was no time for gawking.

Solomon, ever wary, veered away from the trail until the humans couldn't be seen anymore.

The rain continued to pour. The trees provided some relief for the Foxlys as they made slow progress through the thick brush.

The missus barked a warning, and Solomon looked to his left. He was startled to see the mother bear and her cubs climbing the slopes about a hundred yards away. Solomon stopped, and the pups saw the danger too. They whined in fear and huddled close to Solomon. The missus nudged and licked them to try to keep them silent.

The bears lumbered their way up the slopes and out of sight.

Well, thought Solomon, *we're just going to have to take our chances and keep moving.*

He gave Noah and Eli a reassuring lick and began moving through the brush again. The others followed him in a much tighter group.

The windshield wipers on Sheriff Penegar's cruiser seemed to be over-worked from the heavy downpour as he sped from the dam straight to the hospital to help evacuate patients. He also wanted to talk with Tony Harrison about the shooting if the injured farmer was able.

Located on a knoll on the west side of Johnston County, Branton City's hospital seemed too big for the small town. It serviced sev-eral counties and could accommodate over two hundred patients with various degrees of illness. A broad set of concrete steps led up to the modern glass-front entrance with its three sets of double glass doors. Being somewhat elevated above the surrounding area, the hospital would hopefully be spared complete destruction if the dam broke. The beautifully designed structure was a source of pride for the county.

As he pulled into the parking lot, National Guard troops were be-ginning to arrive in their olive-green transport trucks. A grizzled gun-nery sergeant stood in a puddle of water near the hospital entrance, wearing a poncho. He was barking orders to the soldiers as they jumped off the trucks and jostled into platoon formation.

"Forget formation!" he yelled. "Get inside the hospital out of the rain, and start helping the hospital staff with whatever they need."

The soldiers ran up the entrance steps. Orderlies and nurses were holding the double doors open for them as they rushed inside.

Through the rain, the sheriff spotted his old friend Colonel Tucker standing under a wide golf umbrella. Reaching under his seat, he re-trieved a small umbrella of his own, and then shook his head cynically because he didn't think the device was big enough to protect from the wind and rain. He shoved it back under the seat, got out of the cruiser, and ran over to the colonel.

"Hi, Carl." He gave the officer a casual salute.

"Hello, Tom."

"Have you seen Doc Fraley? Has he evacuated everyone?"

"He piled those who could walk into a half-dozen school buses and sent them on their way about thirty minutes ago. There are a number of people still bedridden with IVs and monitors. The four hospital ambulances are going to take the most serious cases, and we're going to transport the rest in the trucks."

"Where are they taking the patients?"

"To the hospital in Ashburg. And, if necessary, the VA medical center in Waynesburg."

"Have you seen Tony Harrison?"

"Tony's a bit weak and on a gurney. He can't go home yet because of the tubes and stuff sticking in him. Clara and one of his sons were with him. I think it was Adam. He helped the orderlies lift Tony into an ambulance along with Clara, and then he got in a car with Tony's old hound and drove back to the farm. The rest of the Harrisons are still there, preparing to let all the farm animals loose in case the water reaches the property line."

"The farm sits on higher ground than the lake. It should be OK," the sheriff mused.

"That's a relief."

"Do you need me here, Carl? I want to check up on Tony."

"No. There's not a lot left to do. The men will take care of transporting those left in the building."

Tom went back to his cruiser and drove off in the rain to catch up with the buses.

— —

Frank Gronsbell stopped the truck in front of the pastor's house. Sonny and Mattie jumped off the tailgate. Mattie ran through the downpour straight for the front door as Sonny thanked Frank for the lift.

"Will the two of you be OK?" Frank asked.

"Yeah. We're going to make it up the Bluff as fast as we can."

Sonny turned and walked toward the house. Frank and his passengers stared for a moment. Frank looked at the others and shrugged. Then he yelled at Sonny. "Get the little girl, and get back on the truck as quick as you can! Get Jerry and Emma, too. We'll make it work."

Sonny looked back and nodded as he joined Mattie on the front porch. He motioned for Frank to wait a moment as Jerry and Emma, along with Allison, came out on the porch. Allison ran to Mattie, who quickly picked her up and hugged her tightly.

Emma said, "We were worried sick about you, Mattie. We've got to get out of here."

"Frank said for all of us to pile onto the pickup. We're heading up to the bluff," said Sonny. "But we've got to hurry."

Jerry squinted out at the truck and said, "We can't all pile on. It's crammed as it is. We'll take our car." He pointed over at the Civic in the side yard.

They all looked at each other, and Sonny motioned for Frank to go on without them. The truck pulled away.

"The keys are in the car already," said Emma.

Mattie carried Allison as everyone dashed quickly off the porch.

They all jumped inside the small car, and Jerry cranked her up. The car pulled onto the road, and they could see Frank Gronsbell's truck in the distance as they headed toward higher ground.

Even though the heavy rain slowed the Foxlys down, they had made good progress up the bluff along with the other creatures trying to reach the top. They were about a third of the way to the top and still in danger of floodwaters when the dam finally broke.

The concrete walls burst with a tremendous explosion that could be heard over the entire county. Millions of tons of water came crashing through the breach, creating a land-based tsunami a half mile wide that swept everyone and everything in its path southward.

Solomon and the missus looked downward and saw the water rushing past the base of the mountain and rising upward.

They barked frantically at the pups to rush up the hill. They seemed to be keeping ahead of the rising water, and all looked safe until Eli, the smaller of the two brothers, stumbled in the underbrush.

Solomon barked for the missus and Noah to keep running as he turned around to try to save Eli.

The water reached the youngster, and he began drifting away with the current.

Solomon rushed toward his son and made the longest and most important jump of his life. He splashed down only feet from Eli. But it wasn't close enough for Solomon to reach him. He watched helplessly as the young fox washed away from his dad and disappeared in the logs and other debris that were moving with the current. Solomon dog-paddled with all the strength he could muster, but it was hopeless. Eli was nowhere to be seen.

Solomon had been rapidly washed a good distance down the Apple. Near exhaustion, he sadly realized he must save himself if the rest of the family was to survive.

He paddled to the right. He was moving with the current and used the momentum to steer toward the far bank. Soon, his rear paws touched the soft mud beneath the water. He let the current carry him near the river's edge, and, with a mighty effort, he scrambled onto the ground.

He shook himself off and looked back upstream to the bluff where he hoped the missus and Noah were still alive.

Then he sat and looked forlornly downstream for a long time, mourning the loss of his son with a high-pitched bark. The sad noise echoed through the woods.

Still sitting on the mountainside, the missus and Noah had been grieving the loss of two family members.

— —

The SUVs with the Scouts were on the interstate heading toward Ashburg when the dam broke. Mr. Barton's car was leading the little caravan. Neither vehicle had been playing the radio so no one was aware of the disaster they had narrowly missed by leaving the campsite early.

Both Scoutmasters' cell phones rang at approximately the same time. The calls were almost identical and were from their frantic wives who had heard about the dam and desperately wanted to know if everyone was safe. This caught the two men off guard and they assured their wives everyone was safe and on their way home. Although in separate cars, both Scoutmasters were thinking along the same lines and told the women to contact all the parents right away and tell them they were going to stop and have each Scout call his folks and let them know they were alive and well. When they hung up, Mr. Thompson was the first to call Mr. Barton and they decided to get off at the next exit.

The men told the Scouts what was going on and the boys began talking excitedly among themselves.

The rain was continuing to pour down when they pulled into a rest area about ten miles later. There were many cars and trucks in the parking lot so the men stopped in front of the service building and told the Scouts to jump out, make a quick bathroom visit and then wait under the shelter next to the building until the SUVs could be parked and the men join them.

After parking a good distance from the service building, Mr. Thompson and Mr. Barton ran over to the shelter. Before they could say anything a man asked, "Are you folks coming from Johnston County?"

Both Scoutmasters nodded.

"I guess you were running from the flood?" said a woman.

Mr. Thompson said, "We just heard about the flood from our wives. How bad is it?"

Another woman said, "The Cherokee Dam broke about an hour ago. It flooded Branton City and almost all of Johnston County."

Mr. Barton exclaimed, "My God. We were on a camping trip on the west side of the county not far from the dam. We decided to leave early." He looked at Mr. Thompson and slowly shook his head in disbelief. Both men understood how close they had come to tragedy.

Another man said, "Marines, soldiers, and helicopters are evacuating as many people as possible."

By this time, Tommy, Alley, Steve, and George had heard further details while in the building and ran back out to share it. They saw the men standing under the shelter and rushed over to it.

"Mr. Thompson! Mr. Barton!" yelled George. "The flood washed over the forest where we were camping!"

Jody and Marty came out and ran over to join the others. All six Scouts were wide-eyed and scared.

Mr. Thompson took out his cell phone and handed it to Jody. "Call your folks, Jody, and let them know you are safe and will be home in a couple of hours."

Mr. Barton did the same thing and handed his phone to George with the same instructions.

After everyone had called home, they piled back into the SUVs and headed for home.

On the way, Jody thought about the bears and the fox and hoped they were alive and well.

— —

At a large open area with acres of flat fields on either side of the highway, the pastor's car caught up with Frank Gronsbell, whose truck had slowed to a crawl due to the traffic ahead. The people in the back of the pickup waved.

It was then that the dam broke. The loud explosion startled everyone on the highway, and traffic came to a complete halt.

At first, no one knew what it was. People got out of their vehicles and looked toward the dam.

In only a few moments, the rushing water could be seen coming straight toward them.

There was yelling and screaming as men, women, and children began running for their lives across the open field on the left, away from the oncoming peril.

Jerry took Emma by the arm and yelled at Sonny and Mattie, "Let's go! Run!" The pastor and his wife began running with the others.

Sonny looked down at little Allison and instinctively picked her up and began running, grabbing Mattie's hand, pulling firmly to make sure the three of them stayed together.

Crowds of people dashed through the open field, many stumbling in the soft dirt.

But it was no use. The water was too fast. It rushed nearer, and the screams became guttural as people realized that imminent doom was upon them. The fast-moving flood poured over them, and they were swept away like so many pieces of straw.

In the turmoil, Mattie became separated from Sonny and Allison. She lost sight of them as the current carried all of them downstream for quite a distance. Mattie was swept toward a section of woods where the tops of tall trees stood above the water. Barely keeping her head above the swirling water, she screamed hysterically over and over, "Allison! Sonny!"

But there was no returning answer. As she washed into the woods, Mattie was acting on pure animal instincts. She grabbed a tree branch and held on, keeping her head above water. For the moment, all she could think about was trying to stay alive. She pulled herself up and stood on the branch and hugged the bole of the tree, not bothering to look up to see that she was near the top. She looked downriver and continued to yell for her lost daughter.

Sonny and Allison washed further downstream. Allison was on Sonny's back, her arms gripped firmly around Sonny's neck and legs around his middle. He swam awkwardly with the current, barely able to keep both their heads above water. He paddled furiously to the safety of a passing log and pulled himself across it. He held on and breathed heavily. He glanced sideways at Allison. "Are you OK?"

He felt her nod against his neck. The log and its human cargo continued to flow with the water.

Most of the traffic on the roads had headed west out of town on the interstate, clearing the way for other vehicles going to the bluff. Those whose cars had been stranded on the far side of the river and others who had not driven to the festival had let the marines hurry them to the school and the waiting helicopters.

The marines had rescued scores of people who didn't have transportation out of the area and were flying them to safety.

Millie and her passengers decided to take their chances and drive the cruiser to the mountain's base. As everyone scrambled out of the car, Millie grabbed the handheld radio.

On foot and moving very fast, they worked their way to the top along with dozens of other people. They joined a crowd that was standing at the south overlook railing, staring down at Branton City in the distance and the Apple River as it flowed away to the southern horizon, when the dam broke.

Everyone stood frozen in silence watching as water rushed around both sides of the mountain. Time seemed to slow down as the floodwaters reached Branton City in the distance. It poured through the town and beyond.

Millie couldn't believe that what she was seeing was real. Houses around the town were uprooted and washed downstream. The conical white steeple of the First Presbyterian Church broke free and toppled into the swirling river and floated away like some kind of gigantic ice-cream cone. Men, women, and children on the bluff yelled in horror as their history washed away. They huddled together, hugging each other for what little comfort they could muster under the circumstances.

Millie held two young teenagers close to her. Together they watched the terrible destruction below, tears trickling down their cheeks.

◄— —►

The sheriff caught up with the caravan of buses and vans carrying hospital patients but didn't try to stop it. He followed it westward for over twenty miles as it made its way toward Ashburg General Hospital and the VA medical facility higher up in the foothills.

While en route, he kept in radio contact with Courtney and Millie to monitor their progress toward safety.

"Courtney? Millie? Where are you guys now?"

Courtney cut in first. Tom could hear the excited voices of the others in the car. "We're pretty far west, heading for Ashburg, like you. We heard the explosion when the dam broke. I think Millie made it to the top of the Bluff."

Millie cut in. "Tom? Courtney? We made it...but all those townsfolk who didn't...God..."

They could hear the pain. Both of them had been trained to deal with trauma associated with large-scale catastrophes, but this was Millie, a lifelong friend. They both wanted to be as gentle as they could.

"Tell us what happened, Millie." Courtney's voice was calm and soothing.

"Well, I'll try, but I probably won't finish."

"It's all right, Millie. We're listening."

Millie calmed a bit and said, "We made it to the base of the bluff along with dozens of other cars. The traffic had come to a standstill. People were getting out of their cars and hurrying up the hill to the top. There were nine of us crammed into the cruiser. We got out in the pouring rain and scrambled to the top with the others and looked over the south overlook wall. There was a long line of cars on the access road below. People were desperately trying to get up the slope. Four of the men in the cruiser ran down the hill to try to help the kids and older folks who were having a slower time of it."

Millie paused and began crying again. "That's when we heard the dam break. It sounded like an explosion. The water rushed around the base of the bluff so fast."

There was another long pause. Millie was crying harder now. "Men, women, children...swept away right in front of us. We watched Branton get washed away. The white steeple on First Presbyterian. Everything we've known about our town."

Millie stopped, and her radio cut off.

"Courtney. Let's let her grieve for a bit."

"I'm crying now too, Tom. Our history—our homes."

"Let's sign off for now. I'll meet you at the hospital in Ashburg later."
"OK."

—◦—

The vast waters of the lake continued to pour through the shattered dam as it emptied. As time passed, the water level gradually diminished.

Sonny and Allison were still being swept along with the floodwaters. Sonny looked down current. In the distance, a large object stuck up in the middle of the river. As it drew nearer, he realized it was the roof of a two-story house. It had somehow managed to jam itself into the soil below the water and embed itself there. Two dormers were on the roof slope.

"Allison! Look! It's a house!"

Allison turned her head and watched. Sonny realized the log would pass by the structure, and he began furiously kicking his legs toward it.

The rapidly moving current dislodged the house from the riverbed just as the two of them climbed onto the roof and held onto the ridge. Allison huddled tightly next to Sonny, who had one arm around her shoulders and one arm slung over the ridge top. Luckily, he was able to plant his feet on the roof of one of the dormers and somewhat relieve his tired shoulders and arms.

They continued moving down the Apple River, this time with a larger craft to carry them. Just how long the house would stay in one piece was another question though.

—◦—

As it had done at the bluff, the water level began to go down where Mattie was still standing on the tree limb. After about an hour, the waters had subsided enough for her to see that she was on the lowest branch of a tall pine tree about fifty feet above the ground.

Since childhood, Mattie had had a paralyzing fear of heights. She almost swooned from the shock of seeing the menacing view of the ground far below and the new danger of falling to her death. With eyes tightly closed and whimpering with dread, she gripped both arms tightly around the trunk and tried to squeeze herself past the bark deep into the heart of the tree. She stood motionless for what seemed an eternity and may have stayed that way indefinitely until someone should happen to come along to save her or she simply passed out from weariness and fell to her doom.

A flashing thought of her daughter broke the dark spell of inertia and gave her courage to face the terrible acrophobia.

I can do this. I can do this, and I can find my daughter, she thought.

With several deep breaths and a conscious effort not to look down, she loosened her grip on the trunk. With another deep breath, she carefully lifted her left leg from the tree branch and wrapped it around the tree. Then she lifted her right leg and wrapped it around. In spite of the dire circumstances, the image of what she thought she looked like made her giggle and blurt out loud to the woods around her, "Pooh Bear! Where's the honey?"

Realizing she would have to move past the branch, she slowly and painfully rotated herself around the trunk, inch by inch.

A surprising thing happened. Concentrating on what she was doing had pushed the acrophobia to the back of her mind, and she began her descent.

She almost slipped and fell several times but finally made it to the soggy ground below. She sat down at the base of the tree to calm herself. She burst out crying again and stood up, yelling out Allison's name to the forest and the river.

She became aware of stinging pain in her arms. Looking at them, she saw that several splinters were stuck under the skin. This took her mind off Allison momentarily as she carefully pulled them out.

She looked up at the sky and shook her fist in defiance. Filling herself with resolve, Mattie picked her way downriver through the mud and debris, determined to find her daughter.

Solomon sat for a long time looking down the river where Eli had been swept away. He finally decided he must get back to the mountain and join Noah and the missus. He cautiously walked back toward the bluff through the mire, ever watchful for larger predators that had survived and were just as hungry as he was. His heart was hung as low as his drooping tail, but he knew he had to keep the family together and move on.

It was close to dusk when he reached the base of the mountain. The water had receded enough that he was able to start trudging up the slope toward the spot where he had last seen his family.

As he drew nearer, he sat down and let out a bark that only other foxes would recognize. It was a high-pitched, soulful bark of greeting mixed with sadness. He waited, but there was no response. He moved further up the slope and howled again.

Higher up, the missus and Noah heard the faint sound and answered back.

Solomon just barely heard them, but that was enough. He continued to bark, unmindful of other animals that were about, as he began running up the hill.

As he neared, his family saw him coming through the trees. All three of them barked excitedly until he reached them.

They nuzzled and licked each other in joy. When they stopped, the reality of Eli's absence rushed in. To try to comfort themselves over the loss, they sat down close to each other on the slope and gazed downriver, full of sorrow for the loss of a son and a brother.

～ ～

The rain had lightened up as Sonny and Allison continued to flow downstream clinging to the roof. They were in the middle of the river, and the current was still strong, but the worst of the rampaging was past. They drifted along for what seemed like hours and many miles. When Sonny looked back upstream, the bluff was only a small dot in the far distance.

He looked at his little companion and asked, "Are you cold?"

Allison shook her head.

"I have no idea where we'll wind up, Allison. Do you?"

Another shake of her head.

They drifted some more, and it became apparent to Sonny that things just might turn out all right. But anything could happen when hanging onto the roof of a house that was floating down the middle of a river in a rainstorm.

Sonny decided to play the game he had played with his own daughter Sara all that time ago.

He gently shook Allison by the shoulders and pointed toward a log drifting by.

"Look! It's an alligator!"

Allison shook her head.

At least she's paying attention, thought Sonny. He said, "Hmm. I think you're right. It might just be a log."

This time, Allison nodded.

He waited a moment, and then pointed at an empty car floating by. "Look at that! It's an airplane!"

Another shake of her head.

Sonny continued to play like this for a while, with Allison alternately shaking her head no and nodding when he finally named the object correctly.

They were floating toward the right shore when both of them spotted something crawling up out of the water onto the bank. It had four legs and was covered in mud when it stood up on the land and shook the water off.

Sonny pointed and said, "Look at that tiny cow!"

And for the first time in her life, Allison spoke to someone other than her mother. "That's not a cow, silly. That's a little fox."

— ~ —

Sheriff Penegar followed the evacuation vehicles into the parking lot of Ashburg General Hospital. The rain was diminishing when he got out of the cruiser and began helping unload the buses. He didn't want to bother Tony Harrison until the old farmer was settled in his room.

Ray Williams pulled up about thirty minutes later. Everyone in his car got out and stretched their joints, which had been cramped tight together for the past hour.

Courtney switched on her handheld radio. "Sheriff? Where are you, Tom?"

She heard the crackle of his radio.

"Over here, Courtney. Look toward the back of the buses."

She glanced over, and he stepped from between them. As she walked over to the buses, Ray Williams, Gene Andrews, and the others from the car followed her.

Tom gave her a huge bear hug as they smiled at each other. Then they stood side by side with Tom's arm around her shoulders and looked at Ray and the others.

Then Ray spoke up. "Tom, I know I speak for everyone who rode up here with me when I tell you that Courtney is the finest, bravest deputy sheriff that you will ever get on your payroll."

Gene Andrews broke in. "Sheriff, she was the very last person to leave Branton after checking every store and building on Main Street for stragglers."

"She kept everyone from panicking. I know she saved dozens of lives," said Roger Hemphill. "We were scared to death and wanted to take off in the car, but we were too ashamed to leave her. She gave us strength."

The men nodded vigorously and agreed out loud.

Once again, Courtney bowed her head in embarrassment, and her face turned bright red.

The sheriff looked at the men, and then at his deputy. "I knew this the day I hired her. Glad all of you could finally see it too."

He squeezed her tight against his side, and then changed tone. "All right, now. Everyone listen up. Let's lend a hand to the soldiers getting all these patients into the hospital."

The group moved to the buses and began unloading the people.

When all the patients had been moved into the hospital, Tom said to Courtney, "I'm not going to interview Tony Harrison right now. I've got to get back to Branton or at least close enough to see the damage. Tony needs rest anyway."

"I'm going with you."

The sheriff looked at her for a moment and then spoke into his handheld radio. "Millie. Can you hear me?"

A moment later, Millie answered, "I'm still here on the bluff."

"Courtney and I are going to try to make it back to town. Maybe you can look down and guide us when we get closer. We're in Ashburg, so it will be at least another hour before we're nearby."

"Tom, I don't want to stay up here anymore. The river has subsided a lot, but most of the roads are washed away. I want to go back home."

"How many people are still up there with you?"

"Most have left, trying to make their way back down the mountain. There are a few of us here. There are a lot of animals scattered around the slope below."

— ~

Millie and other townsfolk wended their way down the bluff to the parking area below. The cruiser and the other vehicles had been washed away, and the road was barely discernable because of the debris and mud.

Millie talked into the radio. "Come in, Tom. The cruiser was washed away along with the road. I'm going to try to walk back to town through the muck."

The sheriff responded, "We've still got a way to go. We'll have to stop about three miles out of town and walk too. The roads into Branton are impassable right now. Why don't you stop at the Coopertown Road and Highway 16 overpass and wait for us? We'll all get together eventually."

"OK, Tom."

"And Millie, uh, be careful, OK?"

Millie looked toward town at the small skyline of buildings. Others had been walking with her, and they helped each other over various obstacles as they returned home.

When they reached the overpass, Branton City was a mile away.

"I wonder what's left of the town," someone said.

"Hard to tell from here," said someone else.

Millie breathed a deep sigh and said, "Well, Tom asked me to wait for him and Courtney. When they get here, I guess we'll walk into town together and see what's gone and what's still left."

The others began moving in different directions toward their homes.

She sat down on a log and waited until almost sunset, when Tom and Courtney finally pulled up. As soon as they got out, Courtney ran over to Millie, and the two women hugged each other closely and cried on each other's shoulders.

The sheriff walked over and stood beside them, putting an arm around each of their shoulders.

Millie and Courtney finally broke apart, and the three friends began making their way through the devastation to their town.

— —

The Foxly family had been among those animals Millie had spoken of, still sitting on the side of the bluff, grieving for the loss of Eli until late afternoon.

But as happens in life, Solomon and the missus knew they must move on and rebuild a lair for themselves. They stood up and began moving down the slope, heading back as best they could toward the creek where they once lived. Perhaps the small cave would still be there, perhaps not.

By the time they had traveled a good distance down its bank, it was dusk, and the waters of the Apple River had subsided enough so that the little stream where they had lived before was once again flowing its own course toward the river.

Solomon led the way through the darkening twilight as the three of them ran to the mouth of the stream and up the creek searching and sniffing for any sign of the cave.

Noah bounded ahead of his mother and father and soon discovered what was left of their home. He turned and began barking excitedly. Solomon and the missus ran to see what he had found.

Darkness fell, and the moon was no longer full, but it cast enough silvery light for all of them to see.

And there it was, a bit ragged from the flood, but it was still home. The hole was half filled with water and mud. Parts of the entrance had been washed away. All three of them began to dig and scratch excitedly until they reached dry earth. By the time they had finished, the Foxlys were too tired to think about how hungry they were, and all three of them curled up close to each other inside the den. The gentle burbling of the creek soon lulled them fast asleep.

— —

Mattie kept close to the water's edge as she continued her journey downriver.

Her determination to find her daughter, dead or alive, kept her panic and despair in check as she stayed focused on her goal while she slogged through the muck and underbrush. She couldn't have known at the time that she had been swept a long way down the river, almost as far as Allison and Sonny, before she had landed in the tree.

— —

Downriver, Sonny and Allison, still clinging to the ridge of the roof, watched as a bridge loomed in the distance. As the house floated closer, they could see it was a railroad trestle with its rusted steel framing and massive concrete piers.

The current steered the house toward the right bank. The house was moving rapidly, and a crash into the first pier was inevitable.

Sonny gripped Allison tighter. "We're going to crash. Hold on to me. If we fall into the water, grab me around the neck again, but don't choke me."

Once again, Allison spoke, albeit briefly. "OK."

The house moved swiftly toward the pier as Sonny and Allison watched in both fear and fascination.

They hit the pier with a resounding jolt that shook the roof violently, but they clung to the ridge and didn't fall into the swirling water.

Sonny could hear loud creaking below the roof. He knew the house was breaking apart, and they needed to get onto the bridge quickly. He scrambled up and stood with his feet straddling the ridge, a foot on each slope. He grabbed Allison by the hand and pulled her up. Swaying precariously and just managing to keep his balance, he bent over, and Allison jumped on his back. Remembering not to choke him, she wrapped her legs around his torso and gripped his neck with both arms.

The house was lodged between the pier and the bank. Sonny wobbled quickly toward the gable end and jumped into the mud about ten feet below. It was a jarring crash to the ground, but the soft earth prevented any major physical damage to either of them.

Allison let go of Sonny's neck and slid down to the ground. He grabbed her hand and scrambled up the bank to higher ground. They both turned and looked down at the house, which was now splitting apart. The roof, which had protected them down the river, broke loose from the upper framing and flipped over in the current. They continued to watch as the roof, now resembling some kind of crude boat, floated away.

They both looked at each other. Sonny held out his hand in a high-five, and Allison slapped it hard. Sonny smiled at her and made a mock grimace and blew on his palm.

"We did it. At least so far. Let's get up on the bridge. If we follow the tracks, we'll come to some town, somewhere," he said with relief.

They started to walk over to the tracks when Sonny felt the pain in his right ankle. He didn't think it was broken, but he knew he had to keep off it for a while.

He looked at Allison and pointed to his leg. "It's sprained, but I don't believe it's broken."

Allison took him by the hand. Slowly and carefully, she led him as he hobbled to the tracks. They looked across the bridge to the other side.

Sonny sat down on a concrete pillar and said, "Let's rest here for a little while. Maybe my ankle will stop hurting soon."

Allison nodded and sat down beside him.

"Are you hungry? I know I am," he said.

"I'm hungry, but it's OK," Allison said.

The pair sat for a long while and watched the river as flotsam and other debris passed by. They were both too tired to play the game Sonny had taught her, and they soon fell asleep, Sonny sitting up against the pillar, and Allison with her head in his lap.

〜

Mattie was beginning to tire, but she pushed onward. After hours had passed, it was late afternoon, and the rain had dwindled to a light drizzle. In the gray light, she saw a bridge in the near distance. Reaching it gave her a short-range goal before she would allow herself to rest. Nearing complete exhaustion, she continued anyway. Her daughter was down the river somewhere, and Mattie was going to find her.

〜

Sometime later, Sonny and Allison were awakened by the blaring air horn of an approaching train. Alarmed, they both jumped up and stood back from the tracks. They held hands as a diesel locomotive came into view on their side of the bridge.

As the engine came nearer, Sonny thought he could get the attention of the engineer, so he stepped a little closer to the tracks. When the train began passing them on its way across the river, Sonny waved his arms frantically up at the figure sitting behind the window. He couldn't tell if the man had seen him or not, and the train, with a cargo of fifty boxcars and tankers, made its way across the bridge safely and disappeared down the tracks on the other side.

— ⁓

Mattie was near the bridge when she heard the train's warning signal coming from the other side of the river. She watched and saw the train as it started across the trestle. She couldn't tell for sure, but she thought she could see someone by the tracks on the far side waving his or her arms at the engine. She hadn't seen another person since she was swept away from Allison and Sonny. Maybe the person had seen them.

She hurried toward the end of the bridge. The locomotive was half-way across when she reached the tracks. She waited impatiently until the engine passed by. The engineer had opened his window and waved to her. She gave a cursory wave back and continued to wait until the last car passed by.

She ran across the trestle, and, as she neared, she saw that the waving man was Sonny. She stopped, and her jaw dropped in total shock. She was momentarily too stunned to speak. Sonny didn't seem to notice her until she finally screamed, "Sonny!"

She stood perfectly still, unable to move for fear it wasn't really him.

Sonny looked across the bridge and was stunned himself when he recognized Mattie. He began waving frantically. Then he looked down at Allison and said, "Your mama's here, Allison! Look!"

Allison ran up to Sonny and grabbed his leg, afraid he might be wrong. She stepped in front of him and saw that the person who had yelled Sonny's name really was her mother. She began running down the tracks, yelling, "Mama! Mama!"

Tears flowed down Mattie's cheeks, and she ran toward her daughter, an ocean of emotion pouring out as she screamed her child's name over and over. "Allison! Allison! Allison!"

Mattie fell to her knees on a crosstie when the two reached each other. She hugged her little girl with all her strength and let herself be engulfed with tears of joy at the miracle of the reunion.

Allison quietly stroked her mama's hair and held Mattie's head close to her small chest and said, "Sonny and I rode down the river on top of a house."

This caused Mattie to laugh out loud through her sobbing. "On top of a house? My goodness!" She wiped her eyes with both hands. "I've never done that before."

"Yep. The house floated away, though, and sank."

Mattie's crying began to subside, and she looked up in Allison's face. She smiled broadly, letting Allison keep stroking her hair as her tears continued. She heard a quiet voice coming from behind Allison. "Hello, Mattie."

Mattie had not noticed when Sonny walked up to them. His soft voice shocked her, and she looked at him standing behind Allison's back.

He looked down at his feet, feeling a mixture of embarrassment and relief.

Mattie's voice was also a mixture. Some of the old resentment and hatred for her stepbrother was there, but her overwhelming feeling was one of gratitude. "You saved my daughter, Sonny. You saved my little girl. I don't know how to thank you."

Sonny remained silent and didn't look at her. Mattie realized he was embarrassed, and she added, "I'm embarrassed too, Sonny. I came back to Branton City for revenge. But there's nothing to avenge anymore."

She reached out her hand to him. He took it timidly, and, with his head still lowered, he said, "I once stood by and did nothing while others robbed you of your childhood, Mattie. I owed you a childhood in return."

He began to cry softly. Mattie pulled him down and put her arm around his shoulder, and the three of them held each other tightly. Mattie said soothingly, "You were too young to help, Sonny. I realize that now."

After a while, Sonny stood up and helped Mattie to her feet. He pointed down the tracks where the train had gone. "Well, the train's going somewhere. There should be a town nearby. Probably Waynesboro. We need to get off the middle of this trestle before another train comes along."

The sleep had helped Sonny's ankle heal somewhat, and he didn't limp as the trio began walking down the tracks.

Sonny lifted Allison up onto his shoulders and pointed over at a fallen log in the woods. "Look, Allison, it's an alligator."

Allison shook her head and said, "That's not an alligator. It's a log."

"Oh. I guess you're right. Must be my eyesight."

Mattie marveled at Allison's newfound ability to talk with other people.

Allison pointed up into a tree at a crow sitting on a branch and said, "Look, Mama, at that big cat sitting up there."

Mattie quickly caught on to the game and said, "Why, that's not a cat, Allison. That's a big, fat crow."

"I guess you're right, Mama. It's a crow."

Mattie was so thrilled at her daughter's talking she could have played the game forever.

It was now dusk, and the sunlight was rapidly dimming. As the last of the daylight disappeared, the waning moon was still strong enough to cast a silvery light on the train tracks and the long path ahead.

As often happens when people are thrown together during a calamity and are forced to help each other survive, Mattie, Allison, and Sonny bonded together in a spirit of comradeship. What could frighten them now?

The trio continued down the tracks, feeling that the worst was over and that something good was just around the corner.

21

The Foxlys slept all night in the lair and awoke with their stomachs growling. Noah whimpered with hunger. Solomon and the missus knew they must find some food. With Solomon leading the way, the three of them set off into what was left of the forest.

The flood had caused widespread destruction over a large area. Trees were uprooted and plant life washed away. The ground was covered with mud and silt.

Solomon looked across the creek. In the far distance was a tree line where the strongest of the flood waters hadn't reached, and beyond that were thick woods.

Solomon knew they had to cross the creek and make it to the forest, where there would be a better chance for hunting prey.

He led the family upstream until the creek narrowed, and all three of them slipped down to the sandy bank. The water was shallow, and there were stones they could hop across to the other side. Solomon went across first and watched as Noah came next. Both Solomon and the missus were keenly aware of the possibility, however remote, that the young fox could fall into the stream and be washed away like his brother, so they tensed themselves, ready to jump in after Noah.

The young fox had no trouble at all getting across with an almost casual hop, skip, and a jump. He turned and, with a self-satisfied smile, sat beside his father and watched as his mother nimbly hopped across.

They climbed the bank and looked at the journey ahead. It was as muddy as the other side, and the going was slow. At several points, Noah's short legs sank in the mud, and the missus had to pull him loose by the scruff of his neck.

The closer they got to the tree line, the firmer the ground became, and the last hundred yards were easy to walk.

They reached the tree line and sat for a bit, surveying the territory. The family could see that the fringes of the flood had run through the forest, washing away much of the underbrush and leaves but leaving the tall trees intact.

Over the years, Solomon had hunted for food in a wide area, and he had hunted here too. He was familiar with where they were and remembered a farmhouse not far from where they sat. It was in a large clearing with acres of fields similar to Farmer Harrison's.

He stood up and stretched. Noah and his mother did the same thing. The family was going on a hunt together again. If there were guns or dogs about, they would just have to take their chances.

The forest was eerily silent. Normally, there would be all the sounds of animals, birds, and insects living together. The flood had killed many of them and scared most of the rest away. The trio padded carefully ahead through the silence, ever mindful of larger predators.

They were nearing the other side and could see the farmland through the trees, when there was a rustling off to the right of them. They froze and looked toward the noise.

In the trees, about fifty yards away, one of the bear cubs was rooting around, looking for food.

All three of them had the same instantaneous thought: *Where is the mother?*

Solomon and the missus knew they must move away quickly, but they also knew they had to remain silent.

Solomon led the way forward in single file with Noah in the middle. They continually glanced at the bear as they made their way to the open field. The cub apparently never noticed them and continued nosing around for food.

The farmhouse was barely visible across a great expanse of flat land. Floodwater had washed away part of the plowed furrows where the Foxlys were standing.

All three of them were exhausted but knew they must move on. A long section of the furrows had been plowed lengthways toward the house, and the family had an easier time walking in one of the troughs. With its walls, the trough could also offer some cover if danger from animals or humans appeared and they needed to crouch down. They also instinctively knew to keep their long tails drooping and out of sight.

Feeling somewhat safer, they began to run, ever mindful of keeping low to the ground. They made it to the end of the furrow and looked across at the farmhouse on the other side of a yard of grass. Over to the left was a barn, and beyond that was a large chicken coop. Was dinner waiting?

Solomon indicated for Noah and the missus to stay where they were while he checked out the grounds.

He carefully padded his way to the house. There was no dog around, which was unusual. If one had appeared, Solomon was prepared to run and lead the dog away from the family. But all was quiet. Too quiet.

There were no humans about. He padded to the barn and looked inside. The stalls had been opened, and whatever animals had been inside were nowhere to be seen.

He padded to the coop and looked inside. It was empty as well. He barked a low call, and Noah and the missus ran to him. The three of them looked around. They didn't know, of course, that the farmer had set all the animals free to escape the flood and left for higher ground with his own family.

What were the Foxlys going to eat? Their hunger was continuing to grow sharper.

Solomon had a hunch. He walked into the coop and jumped up to the nearest nest. Sure enough, there were four eggs in it. He barked excitedly for the others to come inside. The other two ran inside, and each jumped into a different nest. There were eggs enough to feed several families, and the Foxlys devoured dozens of them before they were finally sated.

Full of food and reenergized, the three of them trotted back to the furrow and were going to set off for home when they looked across the field and saw the bear cub. They heard a roar, and the mother bear appeared out of the woods. She stood there and roared again. The cub scampered over to her, and they disappeared back into the trees, apparently unaware of the Foxlys.

Solomon wasn't sure if they would encounter the bears again when they made their way back through the forest. Once again, the family would just have to take their chances.

They couldn't know that the mother bear had also lost one of her cubs to the flood. She was looking for it and feeling her own kind of grief.

The Foxlys trotted briskly back to the tree line and hurried through the woods to the stream. They made their way along the bank to the stones where they had first crossed and hopped over to the far bank.

By the time they got back to the den, the sun was setting. The three of them curled up next to each other and fell asleep almost immediately.

—　—

Monday in Branton City was busy. Tom, Millie, Courtney, and dozens of others who had been spared from the flood spent all day reviewing the damage.

Most of the buildings were still standing but would need massive repairs. First, all the mud and debris would need to be cleaned up before actual renovations could begin.

There was no power, and none was expected for weeks. Many of the businesses and homes had generators, including the sheriff's office.

After cleaning and drying the equipment, most of the buildings on Main Street had temporary electricity. Others, including the Main Street Diner were using candles, flashlights, and emergency lanterns.

The police station was still standing tall, at least as tall as a one-story building can stand. Courtney and the sheriff had been there all night before and had been cleaning up all day.

Millie was across the street. The diner and the bus station had not fared as well. The roof was completely torn off. The benches in the station were washed up in a pile at the front door. Except for the counter stools, which were firmly bolted into concrete, the furniture and supplies in the diner had suffered the same fate as the benches next door.

Millie was over her crying spell and had settled into trying to clean up as best she could.

When the sun was setting, she wiped down the counter and set two candles on it. She went to the cooler and took out a warm bottle of beer. She sat on a stool, lit the candles, and rested.

Over at the station, the sheriff looked at Courtney and said, "It looks like enough for today. Let's go over to the diner and check on Millie."

Courtney nodded in relief. They walked across the street, and Millie got each of them a beer. "They're warm. But what the heck; they're drinkable."

The three of them sat at the counter and gradually began to smile at each other. They were like Mattie, Allison, and Sonny—three survivors who were alive and sitting with each other in comradeship.

When darkness had set in, the sheriff looked up where a ceiling should have been and saw the myriad of stars above.

He nodded his head slowly and said, "Look at the stars, Millie. Seems kind of romantic, doesn't it? Maybe you might think about leaving it that way."

He busted out laughing, and the two women joined him. They drank warm beer together well into the night.

$\sim$ $\sim$

In the middle of the night, Solomon, Noah, and the missus were awakened by a faint noise outside the den.

Startled, the three of them jumped up, ready to bolt in case danger was lurking. They stared into the darkness just beyond the entrance and saw two eyes peering back at them.

There was a whimper—a foxlike whimper. Solomon cautiously moved to the front of the cave and looked out. There was another whimper.

Solomon's heart leaped in his chest. It couldn't be! But it was true. Eli was standing there, bedraggled and muddy but alive. Allison had been right about what she had seen crawl up from the river onto the bank and shake itself off.

By this time, Noah and the missus had come outside. They joined Solomon in a loud chorus of barks as mother, father, and brother swarmed over Eli, nuzzling him and licking his face in joy.

Eli had made it all on his own. As his father had done, he had faced death and escaped its clutches to find his way home. And like his father, he discovered his inner strength and would forever be a leader of his own fox family someday.

After a while, they quieted down and sat together outside the den and looked at the moon. It was continuing to wane, but it still shone bright and familiar.

Just before dawn, they went inside the den and curled up against one another. Soon they were asleep. The Foxly family was whole again.

22

Sonny, Mattie, and Allison walked down the tracks all the way to Waynesboro and were exhausted when they stopped outside the crowded police station. Dozens of families were lined up waiting to get in, trying to get information about family and friends who had been in the path of the flood.

Sonny shook his head at Mattie. "Let's try to find someone in town who can give us a lift back to Branton."

They walked up the street and sat down on a bench. They didn't know anyone in Waynesboro and were too tired to ask around, so they just sat for a while. Sonny was in the middle, and Mattie and Allison leaned against him, all three of them propping each other up.

After a bit, Allison had an idea. "Why don't we make a sign?"

"What do you mean, sweetie?" asked Mattie.

"You know. One of those signs like 'I will work for food.'"

Sonny sat up straight. "Hey, that might work. Wait here, and I'll get us something to write on."

He got up and walked across the street to the local barber shop. In a few minutes, he returned with a scrap of cardboard box. The barber even let him borrow a marker. Together, the three of them came up with what sounded like a sympathetic plea for help. They let Allison write it to give it an innocent child's look.

PLEASE HELP. WASHED DOWNRIVER. NEED RIDE TO BRANTON CITY.

Allison stood at the curb as all three of them put on forlorn and helpless looks.

It only took about twenty minutes before a pickup truck stopped. The driver told them to hop in the back along with two large hogs he was taking to Branton for flood relief.

Sonny looked over the side of the truck bed and said, "Look, Allison, at the two big Jet Skis back here."

Both Mattie and Allison broke into unrestrained laughter as they climbed in with their porcine riding companions.

It was crowded, and the three travelers couldn't help but take turns looking over the top of the hogs at each other and laughing out loud all the way back to Main Street.

When they got there later that evening, Sonny asked the driver to let them off at the sheriff's office. Tom and Courtney were in the office cleaning up. Mattie and Sonny told them the story of their wild adventures on the raging river.

Tom looked at Mattie and at little Allison. "Mattie, I know you didn't shoot Tony Harrison. I was able to talk with him briefly before I came back to Branton, and he said you tried to help him after the shootout with Butch and Bobby. I have a suspicion about who you really wanted to shoot, but no one has seen them since the dam broke. I have nothing to hold you on, so you're free to go."

Mattie gave an audible sigh of relief and began crying when she realized that she wasn't the one who had shot the farmer.

The sheriff looked at Sonny. "Millie and Courtney said you could have skipped town when you left your cell, but instead, you chose to stay and help your stepsister and her daughter. After what the two of you told me about your trip down the river, I think you've paid for your sins out on McAllister Pond Road the other night. You're free to go too."

"There's just one thing, Sheriff," Sonny said. "We don't have any place to stay right now."

Tom offered to put them up for the next few days in two of the jail cells. "Hey. It's not home, but it's dry and has a bed."

The sheriff looked at Allison and winked. "We won't lock you in unless you cause trouble."

Allison grinned back at him.

Courtney got Sonny to help her carry a second bed into Mattie's cell for Allison to sleep on.

After the move, when the three were settled in the cells, Courtney asked, "Do you want anything to eat? The Red Cross and the National Guard have a lot of food for everyone."

"Yes, I think we could all eat something," Mattie said.

Remembering the long truck ride from Waynesburg and the two large animals that accompanied them, Sonny said, "No bacon, though. I think I've lost my taste for pork. For a while, anyway."

Mattie and Allison giggled.

— ❯

Over the next couple of days, Sonny tried to persuade Mattie to bring Allison and see what had happened to the Folsom farm, but Mattie didn't want to go.

He knew she had to confront the past and move on, so he asked Millie to talk to her.

Millie was still dealing with the extensive damage to the diner and the bus station and didn't really know where to begin. She was sitting on an undamaged counter stool when Mattie walked in. Millie got up, and the two women hugged each other for a long time. Millie loosened her grasp and said, "I talked with Sonny. We both know you have some very terrifying skeletons in your closet, Mattie, and they're always going to bother you until you face them."

Mattie looked at Millie. "You know what happened out there, don't you?"

Millie bowed her head. "Yes. A lot of us suspected it, Mattie. And I will go to my grave regretting that I never said anything about it. I need your forgiveness as much as Sonny does."

Mattie took Millie's hands in hers and squeezed tight. "What could you have done? What could any of you have done? I was living with dangerous people. If you had accused them, they probably would have killed me."

They hugged again, and Millie continued. "Skeletons rattling around in the closet are scary, Mattie. But you know what? The problem isn't the skeletons. It's the closet. The longer and harder you try to keep the closet door shut, the louder the rattling becomes. You need to open the door and see for yourself that skeletons from your past are just that—skeletons—dead, harmless bones that need to be dragged out and buried in the past where they belong."

This seemed to allay some of Mattie's fears, and she agreed to go with Sonny to face those skeletons, however frightening they might be.

Transportation was poor. Most of the town's vehicles were flooded or washed away altogether.

The next morning the sheriff borrowed a car from a farmer who had driven into town and who owed him a favor or two. When the sheriff told the man it was being loaned to Sonny Folsom for a very good reason, the man balked. "Sonny Folsom? Are you joking, Tom?"

"Trust me, Drew. Just trust me on this one. I'll guarantee you the car will be back here in a few hours."

Drew looked at the sheriff for a moment, and then shrugged, unconvinced. "All right, Tom. I just want it back in one piece." He reluctantly handed over the keys and walked up Main Street toward the church.

◄ ►

Sonny, Mattie, and Allison drove out to the farm. The nearer they got, the more nervous Mattie became. As they turned onto the remnants of the dirt road leading to the house, she was openly crying.

Allison tried to comfort her. "Mama, nothing bad is going to happen. Sonny won't let it."

This startled both Sonny and Mattie. They looked at each other. They drove for a bit, and then Sonny said, "She's right, Mattie. It's a little late, but let me try to be the big brother you should have had. Nobody is going to hurt you—I guarantee it."

Through her tears, Mattie nodded gratefully.

When they reached the end of the road, all they could see was a flat plain. Nothing was left of the homestead that had haunted Mattie her whole life.

"Look, Mama. There's nothing here to be afraid of."

Mattie slowly got out of the car and stood silently for a long time, looking out over the lonely and deserted expanse. Finally, she nodded her head in a quiet acceptance and turned back toward the car.

Sonny got out of the car and looked around also. After a few minutes, he said "I'm going to sell the land and move on, Mattie. There are ghosts here that haunt me too."

They got back in the car and drove away without looking back. Whatever scary ghosts had been there for all those years were now alone and could not frighten anyone again.

———

On Friday morning two weeks after the flood, two SUVs pulled up in front of the sheriff's office. Mr. Barton, Mr. Thompson, and the six Scouts got out. They were all wearing their uniforms and began pulling brooms, rakes, shovels, and other cleaning gear from the back of the cars and setting the equipment on the sidewalk.

Sheriff Penegar and Courtney had been expecting them. Courtney came out to greet them and said, "Well, hello! You must be from Troop Twenty-One over in Cloverdale. I'm Deputy Sheriff Kruger. Which one of you is Mr. Thompson?"

Mr. Thompson spoke up. "Hello. I called Sheriff Penegar last week and told him we wanted to help with the cleanup."

Courtney shook his hand and then began shaking the hands of the others "We certainly appreciate your offer to help Branton City."

Mr. Barton said "As we told the sheriff, we had been camping in the forest not far from the dam the day it broke. We were very lucky to get out when we did."

The boys couldn't help but notice how pretty Deputy Kruger was, and most of them just shyly stared at her.

The sheriff came out and introduced himself to everyone. "Have you fellas had breakfast yet?"

"We ate before we left this morning," said Mr. Thompson.

Courtney pointed across the street and said, "That's the Main Street Diner. Millie serves breakfast and lunch, when you guys are ready for a break later."

The sheriff looked down the street toward the bridge and said, "We could really use your help in cleaning up the park across the bridge. It took quite a beating from the flood. I know all the townsfolk will be grateful for your generosity."

Courtney added, "There's a group of people over there now cleaning up. If you will join them, I'm sure they can show you what needs to be done."

The Scoutmasters directed to boys to pick up the gear and they moved across the bridge.

The sheriff told Courtney, "Go over to the diner and tell Millie to serve them whatever they want when they break for lunch. The tab will be on me."

Courtney smiled and walked across the street.

— —

Later that day, the Scouts came up the street and marched into the diner.

Millie introduced herself, seated them at several tables, and passed out menus.

Marty opened his and made a show of looking it over very seriously. Finally, he giggled and said to Millie, "Excuse me, ma'am. I don't see roast goose on the menu. Are you out?"

All the Scouts began to laugh. Millie looked a bit confused until Mr. Thompson caught her eye and winked. She understood it was an inside joke and played along. "Why, no, young man. We have been out of goose for several days, now. I'm expecting some in any day now."

George chimed in, "How about bear meat?"

Millie said solemnly, "Why, I believe there just might be some bear meat. The only problem is the bear is still in the woods out back and doesn't take too kindly to being served up for lunch."

"Fox?" asked Jody.

"Fresh out of fox, too. I don't seem to have anything you guys want. Would you settle for cheeseburgers, hot dogs, chili, and fries fixed any way you like?"

Everyone smiled and Millie began writing down the orders. She brought over their drinks and began fixing the food.

The sheriff and Courtney joined them, and the conversation was animated as several of the Scouts related the stories about the thieving fox and the bears.

Later, Courtney asked Mr. Barton, "Where are you staying?"

"We plan to set up a campsite near the old one, if we can still access the area," said Mr. Thompson.

The sheriff said "Yes, the dirt road in there is still passable. Where are you going to clean up?"

Mr. Barton said, "Well, we probably will have to stay a bit dirty for a couple of days."

"When you finish up for today, come into the station, and you can use the jailhouse showers."

The Scoutmasters smiled, and the boys looked excited since none of them had yet to experience what the inside of a jail was like.

"Thank you, Sheriff. I do believe we will take you up on that," said Mr. Thompson. Then he addressed the boys. "OK, men, let's head back to the park."

When he went to pay, Millie smiled and shook her head. "It's on the sheriff. We're all grateful you came to Branton and lent a hand."

After finishing up the day's work at the park, the Scouts were able to drive right to the same location where they had camped before. It needed a general cleanup of debris, but before long the four tents were erected and a campfire was roaring. After sharing different stories and some comments from several of the Scouts about how pretty Deputy Kruger was, the campfire was extinguished, and everyone turned in for the evening.

Late in the night, Jody woke up. Some inner instinct told him to go outside. In order not to wake up his tentmate, Alley, he was careful to be as quiet as possible as he slipped out of his sleeping and went outside.

The campsite clearing was bathed in silver moonlight. He looked around, and to his astonishment, he saw the black forms of four foxes sitting at the edge of the dark woods watching him. There were two large ones and two smaller ones.

Not wanting to scare them off, Jody walked slowly toward the figures. The two smaller foxes and one of the adults stood up immediately and ran into the woods. Jody took another step toward the remaining animal. It stood up but didn't run.

Jody gave the fox a thumbs-up sign and said quietly, "Sorry, fox, no geese this trip. Maybe next time."

The fox seemed to understand. It turned and ran into the forest.

Jody stood still for a few minutes. The hairs on his arm were standing up with the excitement of the situation. He breathed deeply of the clean night air and savored the moment, a personal memory only he could appreciate. He stayed very quiet when he crawled back into the tent and his sleeping bag and fell asleep almost immediately.

Farmer Harrison's farm had been spared. It was located eight miles to the east of the river, and, as the sheriff told the colonel, it was located on higher ground. Tony and Clara returned home three weeks after the flood. Their two sons and their daughter had taken turns to stay at the house until they returned. Most of the farm animals that had been turned loose were rounded up and brought home, even most of the chickens.

Barkley was waiting for Tony and Clara and ran, baying loudly, to the car when they stepped out.

Tony and Clara both bent down low and hugged him tight, letting him slobber all over them.

Tony held the old dog's face with both hands and looked him in the eyes very closely. "You saved my life, old boy. You certainly saved my life."

Clara was stroking Barkley's back with both hands and said, "Yes, sir. It's like they say: dogs are a form of guardian angels."

The three of them walked up to the house together. Later that evening, and for many nights after that, there would be an extralarge bowl of leftovers when supper was finished.

— ⁓

Branton City lost over four hundred souls to the flood. Many bodies were recovered and identified in a makeshift morgue set up in the school gym, one of only a few buildings that were somehow unscathed from the waters. This had been a sad time indeed. Funerals and burials were held daily for two weeks.

Tom and Courtney alternated days, and, between the two of them, they attended every ceremony.

Many more people were gone forever, washed away and lost to the elements.

Bobby and Butch Folsom were among those missing. No one suspected they had fled earlier and left the farm to drown by itself. Nothing was left of the Folsom estate except the land. Whether the truck in which they were riding escaped the river or not, Butch and Bobby were never heard from again.

— ⁓

About a month after the flood, cleanup was still going on. Millie had stood in the doorway of the diner and, along with dozens of shop owners who were posed in their own doorways, watched as a large flatbed tractor trailer slowly and carefully hauled the First Presbyterian Church steeple back home. It had miraculously remained intact during its ride downriver and was found washed up twenty miles below Johnston County. Millie and the others cheered as the steeple passed down Main Street to its home.

Several days later, she joined most of the townsfolk on the church grounds and watched as a crane lifted the steeple to its base on the roof of the sanctuary.

Workers secured it to its rightful place, and the preacher came out on the front steps, where a microphone and speakers had been set up. He urged everyone to join hands in a large circle.

Courtney and the sheriff stood beside Millie.

After the minister had given great thanks to the Lord for bringing so many townsfolk together again, he looked up at the white cone and yelled into the microphone, "Hip! Hip! Hoo*ray*!"

The crowd cheered.

— —

Six months after the flood, Branton City had cleaned away the debris and washed almost all the mud from its face. There was a lot of rebuilding. Homes and businesses that had washed away completely were being erected from the ground up. Life was returning to normal.

Instead of putting a new roof on the diner and the bus station, Millie remembered how nice the stars had looked that first night back with Tom and Courtney, drinking warm beer together. She decided to put a translucent plastic dome overhead. While the contractor waited for it to be fabricated, she had a clear plastic tent assembled and erected over the top of the building to keep out the rain.

One night after the power was turned on, she was sitting at the counter taking a break.

She had brought in her CD player and was listening to some of her favorite albums when the sheriff walked through the door.

"Hi, Millie. Want some company?"

She remained silent, but her smile said it all: *It's about time, Tom.*

He set his hat on the counter and sat down beside her. She went to the cooler and brought out an ice-cold beer. She opened it for him and turned to the CD player. "Do you like Chris Isaak?"

He took a long drink from his bottle. "Can't say I know who he is."

"Can you Texas two-step?"

He set his bottle down and looked at Millie with a sly grin. Then he stood up, unbuckled his gun belt, and set it on the counter. He winked at her and said, "Are you kidding? Watch my moves."

"Wanna dance right here under the stars?" she answered.

The sheriff nodded.

Millie punched a button and looked back at Tom with a smile.

"You Gotta Be Good" started playing. She stood with her hands on her hips, impatient for him to walk over and hold her.

He reached for her, and they danced the two-step up and down the length of the diner. They danced into the darkened waiting room of the bus station. They danced a slow song in the dark and held each other close.

It was the beginning of a romance that had been in the making for a long time.

—　—

It was a full moon. Looking up from the base of the small hill that over-looked Farmer Harrison's chicken coop, one could see the black silhou-ettes of four figures outlined by the moonlight behind them.

The light bathed the coop in its silvery glow.

The Foxly family was hungry, as usual.

Solomon and the missus had decided it was about time for Noah and Eli to hunt on their own, and tonight was the night.

The family had been lying low behind the hill when they first arrived. Solomon had padded quietly over the top and down to the other side, where he crouched and looked for any signs of Barkley or other dangers.

He walked around the perimeter of the coop and looked inside. It was full of plump chickens asleep in their nests. He thought, *Hens tonight! Not eggs.*

He padded silently back up the hill and stood on top, looking down at the others on the far side, who scurried up the hill and joined him. They sat together looking down at the coop.

With a nudge from Solomon, Noah and Eli crept down the hill and moved across the grass to the doorway. They had been warned about Barkley. When they reached the coop, Noah was the lookout and sat peering around the front corner at the farmhouse.

Eli stood motionless at the front door, looking inside for what seemed like an extralong time. He was working up courage for his first solo hunt.

Finally, he rushed inside. The familiar loud squawking started immediately.

As Noah watched, the door to the farmhouse opened, and he saw two dogs running down the porch steps, barking loudly and heading straight for him. A man with a long stick of some kind came out on the porch and looked toward the henhouse. Then the man hurried down the steps and followed the dogs.

Solomon and the missus became alarmed. The dogs were closing in. Solomon made a shrill bark, and Noah ran toward the top of the hill. But Eli was still inside the coop.

He thought about the bear and ran down the hill straight at the dogs. He again was running at top speed when he got near them and then made one of his signature leaps over their heads and landed behind them. The dogs turned and started chasing Solomon, who was now running toward the man pointing the shotgun.

Solomon veered sharply to his left and ran as fast as he could.

Farmer Harrison fired at the fox, but his aim was high, and Solomon just barely escaped into the woods. The dogs gave chase, but Solomon was too fast and left them far behind in the dark forest. He stopped and waited. Then he made a wide circle back to the edge of the woods near the henhouse.

Farmer Harrison was in the doorway looking inside at the chickens. Solomon heard him start yelling as the two dogs ran over to him.

Solomon stayed within the tree line and looked at the top of the hill. The missus was not there. He continued his circle until he could see the back side of the hill. The family was not there either.

He stood still for a while and then made his way back through the forest he knew so well. He was worried, of course. *What happened?* he wondered over and over.

When he finally reached the den, the missus, along with both Noah and Eli, were waiting happily for him. On the ground outside the cave were two plump chickens.

How did Eli manage to grab two chickens? he thought.

It wasn't strength that brought home the prizes. When Solomon ran down the hill to divert the dogs and Farmer Harrison, Noah ran after him and jumped inside the coop to warn his brother. Eli had caught one of the panicked chickens who were flapping around the coop in a riot of squawking and flying feathers. He was standing there with the hen in his jaws when Noah saw him.

Because the barking dogs could be heard moving away from them, the two young foxes realized they could hunt some more. Quick as lightning, Noah pounced and bit down on the neck of an unfortunate hen that had flapped too close for her own good.

They marched proudly out the door, each with a limp chicken clamped firmly in his jaw, and ran back up the hill to their mother.

The three of them watched while Solomon led the dogs on a chase away from them. When he disappeared into the woods, the missus motioned for them to follow her back home.

Foxes are fast studies. Noah and Eli proudly took turns leading them back home through the dark woods. Of course, their mother was there to correct any false paths they might inadvertently take.

And so the Foxly family enjoyed an especially large and delicious chicken dinner. Solomon and the missus were confident that their two sons would be just fine when they finally left the skulk and went out on their own. And it would not be long before they were fully grown and gone.

But for this night, the Foxlys were still together. They curled up in the den after the meal and slept close to each other, happy to be a family and ready to hunt another day.

The End

A Brief History of Foxes

Some background information about foxes may be helpful when reading about Solomon Foxly's exploits.

Foxes are found all over the world. They are native to the entire Northern Hemisphere, including Europe, Asia, and Africa as well as North and Central America.

They were introduced to mainland Australia during the nineteenth century to promote the sport of fox hunting. However, along with the introduction of rabbits during the same time period, this has proven to be an ecological disaster for many indigenous Australian animals. As a result, fox hunting is legal and encouraged throughout the continent, with bounties offered in many jurisdictions.

Solomon came from a family of red foxes. The scientific name for them is *Vulpes vulpes*. They are the largest species of the twelve known "true" foxes and the one most of us are familiar with.

Fox families generally live together in a den that is sometimes called an "earth," a "leash," or a "skulk." It is often a hole in the ground or the side of a hill with several exits in case danger strikes.

Foxes are fast. Very fast. An adult fox like Solomon can run up to forty-five miles per hour. That is almost as fast as the blackbuck antelope, one of the world's fastest animals.

Foxes have a surprisingly large vocabulary of barks and sounds they use to communicate with each other. These sounds can be classified into yells, shrieks, whines, "ratchet" calls, staccato barks, the colorfully named "wow-wow" barks, yodels, growls, coughs, and screams.

When attacking, foxes leap high in the air and pounce down on their prey, much like cats do. In fact, foxes and cats have a lot in common. The pupils in a fox's eyes are vertical, the same as a cat's, to make hunting at night easier. Some species have retractable claws like a cat's and can climb trees.

They have incredible hearing. A healthy mature fox can detect the ticking of a watch from forty yards away—almost half the length of a football field.

Like a few other animals, foxes seem to be able to use the magnetic north pole when hunting. In deep snow, foxes have been known to detect the movements of small rodents on the ground three feet below the surface. When randomly hunting in snow, a fox will be unsuccessful most of the time. However, when it aligns itself with the magnetic north pole, its success rate climbs to 75 percent. A fascinating video of this process can be seen on Youtube.com.

Foxes have been with us for thousands of years. Hopefully, they will be around for thousands more to come.

Acknowledgments

I have many people to whom I owe a debt of gratitude for helping me bring this story to publication.

At the top of the list is God. I am very grateful for the doors that have been opened for me and the direction my life has taken for the past thirty-seven years.

To my son, Dana, for encouraging me to complete this book. Without his love, good wishes and gentle chiding, I would never have finished.

To my daughter-in-law, Emily, and her mom and dad, Cindy and Al Yount, for so many good things they have shared with all of us.

To my oldest and closest friends, Jack Hemphill and his wife, Barbie, for inspiration and positive feedback. Jack has four wonderful novels under his belt, and I need to catch up.

To my brothers, Richard and Eric, for our lifetime of love, loyalty and encouragement.

To Peggy for laughing together and keeping me relatively humble for all these years.

To Barbara Grainger for her invaluable help with my initial editing.

To my counselor, Mary Bobis, for helping me unblock and move forward.

To my good friends in the Men's Group—Tony, Jim, John, Monte, and Scott—for just being there for the past twenty-something years.

To Scott Robinson and the rest of my magic buddies in Sleight Club. Never underestimate the creative imagination and just plain fun a magician can offer to a writer's arsenal of ideas.

To Chris and Robin Neville and Terry Shiels, three of the finest photographers and videographers in the business for all the stimulating times when we shared experiences and ideas.

To Eric and Susana Morris, the greatest acting teachers in the world, for helping me face my fears and expand my mind.

To Mary Anne Beaty and Bob McRorie at RJMW, along with the entire claims department at PURE Insurance for providing me with the financial means to work on my writing.

To Angela and the staff at Forward Design and Print Company, who listened to my ideas for graphics and delivered exactly what I wanted.

To my personal editors and the entire staff at CreateSpace for their knowledge, expertise, and insight. Investing in their program was a bargain and just what I needed—seasoned, objective views on how to make the overall story as well as Solomon and all the other characters richer and more fascinating.

About the Author

Komadori Photography 駒鳥
Robin Neville

illy Haake lives in Waxhaw, NC. He is a U.S. Marine Corps Vietnam veteran and a cancer survivor. He has written articles and short stories for various publications including *Magic Magazine* and *The Linking Ring* and is currently working on a full-length screenplay.

Solomon Foxly is his first book.

Made in the USA
San Bernardino, CA
13 December 2017